MW00436930

CHARLIE
Zombie Slayer
Book 1

GAYLE KATZ

Copyright © 2019 Gayle Katz

All rights reserved. No part of this book may be reproduced in any form, stored in any retrieval system, or transmitted in any form by any means—electronic, mechanical, photocopy, recording, or otherwise—without prior written permission from the author. For permissions contact:

gayle@gaylekatz.com

This is a work of fiction. Names, characters, places, and incidents either are the products of the author's imagination or are used fictitiously. Any resemblance to actual persons, living, dead, or undead, businesses, companies, events, or locales is entirely coincidental.

Visit the author's website at GayleKatz.com.

ISBN: 9781079276022

TABLE OF CONTENTS

Prologue	1
Chapter 1	3
Chapter 2	13
Chapter 3	25
Chapter 4	38
Chapter 5	51
Chapter 6	64
Chapter 7	77
Chapter 8	90
Chapter 9	102
Chapter 10	114
Chapter 11	125
Chapter 12	138
Chapter 13	150
Chapter 14	163
Chapter 15	172
Chapter 16	187
Chapter 17	196
Chapter 18	209
Chapter 19	221
Chapter 20	234
Epilogue	246
About the Author	251

PROLOGUE

Charlie held her hunting knife at the ready. She was glad she'd wrapped the handle with leather, as it made it more comfortable to hold for extended lengths of time. It also made it easier to grasp when she had to plunge the tip into the head of her prize. She heard a crackle and quickly ducked behind one of the headstones in the cemetery.

Her mentor had texted her the info at 2 am, so she'd quickly put on her sweats and running shoes, grabbed her backpack—already filled with gear—and hopped into the VW Beetle that her dad had left her in his will.

The crackling sound continued. She raised her head and breathed deeply. Soon it would be time to kill.

The crackling sounds turned into dull footsteps. Something, or someone, dragged their feet across the ground. Small pebbles and plant debris went cascading in all directions.

When she was ready, she leapt out at the creature. She lifted her dagger high into the air and struck.

The knife slipped easily through the eye socket and into its brain. She briefly winced, knowing that this was far easier than killing a human. She didn't even want to remember that detail.

The creature made a gurgling sound, and then dropped slowly to the ground.

"Dammit! Now I have to clean up." She cleaned the filth from the dagger as best she could, rubbing it against the dirty pants of the dead body at her feet.

She walked around the carcass, lifted it by the armpits, and dragged it to the nearest hole in the ground.

It took her only a few minutes to fill in the earth.

"There, that's done," she commented. "Now I'll look forward to retirement."

CHAPTER 1

"Welcome to Portland High. We hope you'll like it here. We're a very welcoming and diverse community, unlike that state you're from," said Principal Allan.

"Are you serious? You mean Texas?" Charlie commented. "It's all right. Every place has its bad apples."

"Of course," said Allan. "We heard you've come here with a reputation."

Charlie glared at him. The smile left his face.

"Well, that concludes the guided tour. Your first class is biology with Mr. George."

Charlie stopped walking. "Mr. George?" she asked. "I hope that isn't Stewart George."

"Why yes, it is. You know each other? I hope you don't have a problem with him. He came highly recommended." Principal

Allan smiled an awkward smile.

"Yes, we know each other. And yes, I like the guy. It's just that he was also my bio teacher in Dallas. It's odd that he moved at the same time as me." Charlie looked around the hallway, a worried expression creeping onto her face.

"Oh, that's quite the coincidence. Then you'll settle in here much faster than I expected." Principal Allan gestured at an open door. "This is where…" he started to say, but couldn't finish because Charlie was gone.

Charlie stomped angrily into bio class. Mr. George looked up at her and smiled, a smug expression on his face.

She glared at him, and went to the back of the class, choosing a desk. She smashed her backpack onto the ground.

"Hello, class," he said, beginning the day. "We have a new student today. Her name is Charlie Warner, and she's from Dallas, Texas. Please say 'hi' to her."

The entire class said "hi," except for Zan. She sat in the front row, her eyes reading her smartphone.

"Hi, everyone," said Charlie. "I'd sell you drugs at lunch, but I hear that you can buy them at any store in Oregon now." That got a chuckle out of the majority of students, except for Zan.

"Drugs are bad for you," Zan said, putting her phone down.

"OK, class, let's get started on the lesson for today."

The day was your typical 11th grade experience. Charlie did her best not to interact with anybody. When she could, she glared at Mr. George. Finally, first period ended. She remained behind.

When the class had departed, Mr. George closed the door.

Charlie grabbed her things and stuffed them into her backpack. She stormed to the front and slammed it onto his desk.

"Why are you here? I told you that I'm done. Seriously, I'm done."

"Please calm down, Charlie. There are things that are out of my control. I told you before that this is a lifetime thing."

"I don't want a lifetime. I just want to lead a normal life." She grabbed her backpack and headed to the door.

"Wait," called Mr. George.

Charlie turned to face him.

"I know that you put down the southern

gang, but unfortunately, we have a new problem in Portland."

"That's just great," she said, but she didn't move closer to the door.

"Apparently, a tourist from Portland visited her great-grandmother's grave in Dallas. Unfortunately, she was bitten."

Charlie dropped her bag. "Wait. Tell me she did not come back to Portland."

"Yes, that's just it. And it's worse."

Charlie shook her head and kicked her bag.

"She wasn't bitten by just any zombie. If so, someone would have taken her down immediately. But they didn't realize. She was bitten by the zombie leader."

Charlie shook her head, trying to take it all in. "But I killed the zleader. She's gone."

"I know. But, apparently, she was bitten by her in the cemetery, then she holed up in the ground for a while."

"Oh no," she cried.

"Right," said Mr. George.

"But if she was bitten by her, and I killed her, and then she came back here to her city…" her voice trailed off.

"Right. That means she is a new zleader."

"Crap," said Charlie. She picked up her

bag. "Anyway, I'm late for chem."

"I'm sorry. I had to intervene," her teacher said.

"I know," she said, reaching for the doorknob.

Mr. George tidied some papers on his desk and placed them into his briefcase. "So, are you in, or what?"

She turned and glared at him. "What do you think? That I'm going to let the zombies eat up the city?"

"Good. Let's meet at 3 pm, here."

"Fine," she replied. "But I'm telling you, when this city is clear, I'm truly done."

Mr. George nodded. "I know. I'm sorry you killed a human by mistake. I've done the same. It never gets easier."

"Right, I forgot that you had too." Her voice grew softer. "I'm off to class now."

"See you later," said Mr. George. "Oh, and it's Mr. George here, not Stewart. As far as anyone knows, I'm your bio teacher, not your mentor."

ZZZ

Chem class went well. Charlie was able to focus on the elements and chemical formulas and forget about the problems looming ahead.

She had nearly made it through class without interacting with anyone. The last thing she wanted was to make friends, only to have them gruesomely eaten up by zombies. Sadly, that's what happened when you hung out with Charlie.

"Psst," called the guy beside her. "What is Au again?"

"Gold," she whispered back.

"Thanks," he said. "I'll try to remember that."

Charlie couldn't help but smile at him. He seemed like a truly nice guy.

The bell rang, and the class was done. For once, she felt a bit disappointed.

"Hey, you want to hang out at lunch?" he asked. "I'm Owen Nakkonde, from Uganda."

She stood up and shook his hand. "Hi, Owen. I'm Charlie. Nice to meet you." For some reason, she couldn't be her usually snarky self. "Umm, sure, I'll see you in the cafeteria." She supposed she could have at least one friend at school. She'd just make sure that he never found out what her true calling was, or else he'd be in danger too.

There was one more class until lunch, English. She sat beside Zan, the same girl from her bio class. Zan tried to avoid looking at her as much as possible.

"Oh darn, I broke a nail," she commented at one point.

"You're lucky you have nails," said Charlie.

"What did you say?" snapped Zan.

"Zombies don't have any nails," explained Charlie.

Zan frowned at Charlie's casual wear, and then glanced down at her linen jacket and skirt that had taken her half an hour to iron that morning.

"Oh, you're one of those zombie film buffs," she commented.

"Yep," said Charlie. "I'm really good with a gun and a knife too."

The bell rang. Zan grabbed her things and quickly left.

"Hey, see you later," Charlie called after her. She had a good chuckle. There was that old saying to keep your friends close and your enemies closer.

zzz

"Hey, over here!" called Owen.

Charlie set her tray on his table.

"How's your day been?" he asked.

She was about to lie and say it had been terrible, but surprisingly, different words came out of her mouth. "It's been good, actually."

"Fantastic! I think you'll like it here. I went from being bullied at another school to being openly welcomed here."

Charlie shoved her sandwich into her mouth. "Seriously? Let me know who it was and I'll whoop their ass."

"Really? That's great, from a girl and all."

Charlie frowned at him.

"I mean, girls, err, women, can do anything a man can."

"You got that right. Anyway, if you want some tips, I can help teach you to defend yourself."

Owen smiled at her. "That'd be great, as I really have no idea. I'm such a wuss. Well, I am a truthsayer, so sometimes I have the disadvantage."

Charlie spit a piece of lettuce out of her mouth.

"You're a truthsayer?"

"Yep. You know, I have to tell the truth, and I influence others to tell the truth too."

Charlie looked worried. "Like, a superpower or something?" She took a sip of her milk.

"Nah, nothing like that."

But she doubted him. She was looking forward to meeting up with Stewart later to ask questions.

"So, how about that Zan?" she asked him.

"Oh, the rich girl. She acts grumpy, but she's OK."

"Nothing to worry about then?" Charlie wanted to smack herself. She had made a promise not to get involved in school dynamics again, and here she was making friends and asking questions.

"Nah, she's fine. Makes stupid comments sometimes. She won't openly say anything bad though."

"Well, I'll steer clear of her. She's not into zombies anyway." Oh crap! Why did she say that to him? She wanted to stay quiet about the zombies. Some people in the city knew about them, but most called them an urban legend.

Owen's eyes grew big for a bit. It was like he wanted to say something, but then didn't. "Hey, serious stuff. Let's just talk about TV shows or something."

Charlie smiled and continued eating her lunch.

CHAPTER 2

Charlie and Stewart were in his bio class, lights off and the door closed and locked.

"What do you mean I have to go into the field tonight? I just drove into town with Gran yesterday! I don't even get two days off?"

"Calm down. This is a simple zombie sighting. My sources have told me that there has been some activity off Main Street in a back alley. So far, the bitten have been taken down, but no one has been able to find the zombie yet."

Charlie paced the room. "Well, maybe the zombie is the zleader? You expect me to just wander in and take down a zleader? I have to prepare. I can't just walk in."

"No, we don't believe it's the zleader. Unfortunately, she has already infected others," explained Stewart. As he talked,

Charlie noticed a map of the city on his desk with highlights in red. "We'll have you go in, do some control first."

"Fine. But do you have any idea where the zleader is?" she asked, continuing to pace the room.

"No, but I'll let you know as soon as we do."

"OK. In the meantime, I'll prepare for a zleader attack. Going to have to find supplies and gear up."

"Good plan, Charlie. I'll see what I have in storage so you don't have the expense."

She raised her arm in the air and waved. "Told you before, money is no object since Gran won the lottery."

"Still," he started saying. "I'd feel more confident that you had the right equipment, than buying from some questionable Portland occult store for the tourists."

She nodded. "Oh, and I had a thought."

Stewart looked up.

"When I was fighting the zleader in Dallas, she seemed to show fear when my ring touched her arm."

Stewart frowned. "That's interesting. I know werewolves are sensitive to silver."

"No, the ring is titanium, not silver or

gold."

"Ahh," said Stewart.

"Is it possible to have a dagger made from titanium?" she asked him.

Stewart grabbed his tablet. "Well, anything's possible. However, it may take time. And I'm concerned about its strength. You may only have one strike with it."

"Well, that's all I need."

"Fine," he responded. "But I still think you should have your usual too."

"Yep," she said.

"Oh, and we'll need to enchant it, just like the others," said Stewart.

"You mean, with a spell?" she asked.

"Yes. I've been reading up on spells. It's not quite my specialty, but if I learn more about them, then we can benefit. These zombie leaders seem to be evolving and becoming smarter. There is also the concern that they, too, can utilize spells, so it's important for me to place protections around the spell book, and to also enchant it for only the eyes of the living. Not only that, but there may be ways to help protect people's houses. The downside is that the spells take time and focus only on a small area of protection, such as a house. There are also spells that can increase the power of an object, such as the killing power of a dagger."

"Do what you have to do," she said impatiently. "Well, I guess I should get going. I'll have just enough time to grab dinner with Gran, and then hop on the bus to get to that alley."

"Bus? I thought you brought your Beetle?" He snapped his tablet case closed.

"No parking downtown, remember?"

"Right, so anything else?" he asked. "I need to think about dinner too."

She grabbed her backpack and was about to head to the door when she remembered something. She turned to face him.

"Is a truthsayer a thing?" she asked him.

"Why yes, they're similar to a zombie slayer, a person with superpowers, if that's what you're asking. Why? Did you come across one?"

Charlie was hesitant to tell him about Owen until she knew more. "I might know someone who is one. I don't think he knows. Are they harmful?"

Stewart sat down. "Well, basically no. They have powers that can be helpful to fight zombies. However, the bad guys can also use them, as they aren't good at the art of deception. So, if you've met someone like this, I suggest that you don't tell them the truth, and steer clear."

"Right," she said. "Pretty much what I figured." She left and headed for home.

On her way home, she felt like she could really use a friend. Not just Gran, who was like a mother to her, but Owen, her new friend. She'd just have to learn how to control her mind so that she wouldn't blab anything. She was also curious as to what kinds of powers a truthsayer could have that would help with zombie fighting.

zzz

Charlie stepped off the bus at Main Street Books and longingly looked at the store. If only she could simply go inside and do book shopping like a normal person. Most people were oblivious to the fact that there were magical creatures, like the zombies, who mysteriously reanimated after death. They gained their power from feeding on the living.

She checked her map and headed down the block to the back alley where zombies had been sighted. There was some gangland graffiti on the walls. She stared at it, but none of it seemed zombie-related. The zombie gang in the south had actually painted strange symbols at their headquarters. She assumed that a new gang of zombies would likely use the same symbols, but couldn't see anything out of the ordinary.

Charlie walked straight down the alley. If there were any zombies lurking here, she might as well get it out of the way. As she walked, she smelled a putrid scent floating through the air. She abruptly turned left and headed to a silver trash can. Sure enough, inside was what appeared to be a dismembered human, or what was left of him anyway. She definitely was on the right track.

She headed back down the alley and whistled and sang, being certain that whoever was lurking in the distance knew that she was only a small, unassuming female.

Someone was there. He came out of the shadows. He wasn't too far-gone yet. The only clues that something was amiss were that he was missing his shoes, and the bloodstain around the lower part of his face. Looking at his head, she noticed his eyes glowed green. His arms reached out for her with that distinctive zombie stance.

Two seconds later, he'd been stabbed through the head and was lying dead on the ground, for the second time. She dragged the body into a large dumpster. In her experience, only the homeless sorted through the trash cans and dumpsters and they didn't say anything when there were dead bodies in there, as that could indicate guilt. Unfortunately, a lot of good people went missing that way too.

She did two more rounds of the alley, even checking behind the dumpsters and trash cans, but she found nothing. She was standing in the middle of the alley when she heard something. It sounded like someone was pounding on a window.

She glanced behind her. Just as she reached for her dagger, the zombie smashed through the glass window and launched himself at her.

"Stupid move! Now you've attracted everyone's attention!" she cried. It took only a moment, but soon he was dispatched. She moved his body into the large dumpster. She heard voices in the distance.

She would have left right then, but where there were two zombies, there would be more. She hopped through the broken window, just as people came into the alley. She squatted down and watched. It appeared to be tourists. They had a peek, and then decided to leave. Wise move. If there were any more zombies here, they'd quickly be avocado toast.

When they were gone, she grabbed a flashlight out of her backpack and turned it on. She shined the light around the tiny room, revealing what appeared to be a small entryway. There were stairs, so she walked up them. Once upstairs, it appeared to be a normal apartment dwelling. She lightly padded down the hallway, trying each doorknob. They were all locked. That was good news as it meant that the zombie hadn't been able to bite anyone.

Zombies were relatively stupid. They could push or pull their weight, but they couldn't figure out how to turn a doorknob or use a key. That meant that the guy probably had been bitten hours earlier and had just happened to be near the exit when he turned.

There wasn't much happening here, so she went back down the stairs, the only way out. She slipped out the window, and then heard someone in the building walking down the steps. She hid behind one of the trash cans.

She watched as a man left the building. She abruptly jerked her head back when she saw that it was Principal Allan. What on earth was he doing here? Was it possible he lived in such a rundown building? Highly unlikely for a high school principal who probably got paid in the high five figures.

She watched as he walked down to Main Street and headed for a parking garage. There was nothing to do but follow him.

zzz

Charlie had to check in and out whenever she was on location. That was the rule between her and Stewart. She pulled her cellphone from her pocket and dialed him.

"Hi, Charlie! How is the gig?"

"Fine. I killed two, and saw one dead human."

"Great, err, I mean about the zombies," he replied.

"Do you know where Principal Allan lives? I saw him leaving this location."

"Really?" asked Stewart. "That's odd. I think he lives in Vancouver. I can't think why he'd be in that part of town, unless he was visiting the book shop."

"He was nowhere near the books," Charlie said.

"Well, check it out and keep me posted."

"Will do," she said, folding the phone and jamming it back in her pocket.

zzz

So far, surveillance had been fairly boring. She peered at him through the bushes. Principal Allan looked to be in no shape or form, a zombie. A zombie leader could mask as a human, but their eyes would still glow green.

She watched as he entered a coffee shop. There's nothing odd about that. She wanted to give up, yet she felt that she was missing something. She was seriously ready to head home and do her homework, but she needed to find out what was going on. She decided to take the most practical tactic.

Charlie walked right into the coffee shop, like she just happened to be in the area.

"Hey, Principal Allan, fancy running into you here," she said, as he sat at a table sipping a drink. Startled, his head and shoulders lurched forward abruptly. Seated across from him was a woman, obviously, not his wife.

"Oh. Hi, Charlie! I'm just here chatting with my friend." But he didn't give her name.

"Great! Sounds good. I'm going to check out the bookstore before it closes tonight." She ordered and received her drink.

Allan watched her carefully. He seemed a bit disturbed that she decided to hang around and take a seat near the wall.

Charlie listened to their conversation, but most of it seemed like small talk. They talked about school curriculum and the weather. She finished her coffee and tossed the empty cup into the trash can. She waved at the principal and headed near the door.

But, instead of leaving, she ducked into the bathroom.

Charlie quickly did her business, and then she slowly opened the door up and peered around the corner. He was still there with his friend.

She could make out some words. It sounded something like, "zombie drugs" or "zombie deal."

She remembered when she worked at a small store in Dallas and there had been talk among the staff about someone's son taking a zombie drug or something.

But then they suddenly got up from their seats, so she ducked back into the bathroom. When she was certain they were gone, she left the shop and headed for the bus stop. She'd have to quiz Stewart to see if he knew anything about this zombie drug. Hopefully, it had nothing to do with zombies, but on the other hand, if it did, it could be extremely dangerous.

CHAPTER 3

It was back to biology class again, but Charlie showed up early before the students had a chance to arrive.

"So, do you have my new dagger yet?" she asked Mr. George.

"What do you think?" he retorted.

"Whoa, I'm only joking," she said.

"Sorry, it was a long night. I had to do some investigating. But at least we have more to go on."

"Good, any steps closer to finding the zleader?" She went to the back of the classroom and dropped her backpack on the floor.

"Maybe. There's a place I want you to check out after school." Mr. George consulted the map on his desk. "It involves buying drugs."

"Wow, only three days in town and I'm a

druggie," she said jokingly.

"Right," he said, not really paying attention.

"Do I have to do it right after school? I'm supposed to show Owen some self-defense moves."

"Oh, you can bring him along."

Charlie dropped her pen on the desk and stomped up to the teacher's desk.

"What are you saying? I'm not going to put a civilian's life at risk."

He lifted his head and looked at her. "I thought you said you were teaching him self-defense."

"Well, yeah, but it's so he can beat up bullies, not zombie-dealers."

"Fine. Go alone then. But the usual rules apply."

Charlie adopted a slightly self-righteous smile on her face and nodded. "Great. I'll go after I teach him some moves." She went back to her desk and sat down.

"I thought you weren't into zombie games anymore?" Mr. George asked her.

She glared back at him. "Well, as it turns out, there is nothing to do in this town, so it gives me something to do."

"Nothing to do? We're in Portland,

Oregon. There is a world-class art gallery just a few steps from us. There are theatres, shopping, and arcades. Or you could just do your homework."

"Nah," she said.

Just then, they heard footsteps coming closer. It was time to can the conversation and focus on schoolwork. The first student through the door was Zan.

"Hey, someone's early to class. Usually it's me." She took her seat at the front of the room.

ZZZ

Charlie met Owen on the field after classes were over.

"Now, stand sideways, as there is less for an attacker to grab onto."

"Like this?" he asked, turning sideways.

"Yep. And hold your arms up like this for defense. You can use them to deflect a blow. While they can get hurt, a stab wound won't kill you like it would if they reached your heart."

"Stab wound, whoa! The meanies from

my other school don't have knives," he said, protesting.

"Seriously, Owen. What country do you live in? Of course they have knives! Watch the news!"

"OK. OK," he said, getting back into his stance.

"What do you do if someone grabs you by the neck?" she asked.

"Hey, I know this one!" He placed his hands together in a prayer position, and then lifted them up into the air. Then he swooped down on both sides, knocking her arms away from his body through pure weight and gravity. Then he jumped back.

"Good!" she said, pleased. "You already know this stuff. It's just a matter of practice."

"But, what happens if I freeze?"

"You won't. Your instincts kick in, fueled by adrenaline," she explained.

"Hey cool!" he said, raising his fists up into the air and jumping around the field. "Now I'm protected from a zombie attack."

This made her pause. She wondered how much he really knew.

"Hey, you OK?" he asked her, putting his fists back down and ceasing movement.

"Sometimes you get too quiet."

"Oh, it's not you. I have a lot on my mind." There, she did it. She didn't blurt out the truth. She did have some sort of magical protection. She was a zlayer after all. "I lost my parents a few years back. And it's like I have to be an adult now."

"I know what you mean. I have a part-time job to help support my family. Dad says I don't have to do it, but I know I do. It helps to build our savings so I'm not such a drain on my parents when I go to college."

"Yep," she said. "Oh, there's Zan. Night, Zan!" she called out to her as Zan climbed into her BMW. "Geesh! A BMW. Her family must be loaded."

Zan looked back at them and waved.

"She's been less on the jokey comments lately."

"Well, it does get old after a while," said Charlie.

"Well, time for me to get home," said Owen. "Thanks for the tips! Let's hope I never ever have to use them."

"I pray that you won't ever have to use them either," she said.

As she headed to her own car, she wondered why Zan had stayed late after school. She wasn't the type of person who'd be in detention or who'd need special attention for a math problem or project.

As she drove around the back of the school, she saw Principal Allan leave the building. Odd. Why would he stay late too? Of course he was the principal, so they must put in overtime, but the hairs standing up on the back of her neck said that something was up. Could that be the reason why Zan had stayed late?

zzz

"Hi, Gran," said Charlie to her grandmother.

"Hi, dear. Dinner is almost ready." Gran was making lasagna and had just taken it out of the oven. "Are you going to the library again tonight?"

"Yes, I am," said Charlie. "Got a big project to do. But I'll only be away for a couple of hours."

Gran knew that Charlie was a zombie slayer, but Charlie never brought it up and neither did Gran. She simply accepted that she had a strong female granddaughter and tried to guide her along as best she could, even if the cops dropped her off at home a few times, or she had a few bruises on her arms. She trusted her to look after herself.

They only had each other, so Gran also knew Charlie didn't want her to be placed in danger. That had happened once, back in Dallas. That was one reason why Gran had pushed for the move to Portland, in fact, or at least a robbery had been the cover for it.

After Charlie had killed the zombie leader, the city and even the state were fairly safe from zombie gangs for at least a few months. There was no one left to target them there, but Gran knew Charlie had been tired of fighting and wanted to lead a normal life.

That's why when the police had dropped Charlie back at home one night, saying that she had been attacked by a gang, but had fended for herself, Gran knew it was time to make a change. After that, Charlie had agreed with Gran to move to Portland.

Now on the same page, they sold their house in Dallas and bought a new one in Portland. Unfortunately, Stewart must have figured it out, and followed them there after he learned of the danger that Portland was now facing.

Gran frowned thinking about Charlie and her obligations. Of course there was no one else in Dallas, and now Portland, who could fight zombies, except for a few random cops. She sighed.

"Dinner is ready," said Gran.

zzz

Charlie was in another dark alley, awaiting instructions. She held her cellphone close to her, with a large dagger in her right hand. Her phone rang.

"Hey, Stewart," she answered.

"OK, so my sources say that you head for the sign that says FORTUNES FORETOLD, and that's where they're selling drugs."

"Right," she answered. "But I'm not looking for weed or coke, or bath salts."

"Nope, this is a new drug. It's believed that it's manufactured from zombie blood and has a street name of zrug, at least that's what I'm told."

She kept up her watch outside. "Figures. Wait, if it's made from zombie blood, then wouldn't drug users who take it also turn into zombies?"

"Not quite. It's heated to a certain temperature to destroy the virus, but not enough to destroy its magical properties. Apparently, the drug has an effect on the user's brain," explained Stewart. "We're not quite sure what yet. I'm in contact with a coroner who's dissecting a human who took too much of it."

"Yuck," Charlie commented. "Sounds worse than bath salts or meth."

"It is, because long term usage leads to death," said Stewart.

How ironic, Charlie thought to herself. Instead of turning you into a zombie, all the zombie drug did was kill you. "OK, so, you want me to figure out if they're dealing?" she asked.

"Exactly. Good luck." He hung up.

Charlie muttered to herself when she was annoyed. Why didn't they send a cop to do the dirty work? Why send her? A cop could raid the joint. Well, here goes.

She walked up to the brightly painted, but extremely chipped, front door of the residence and knocked.

The door slowly swung open. A woman stood there, not wearing a lot of clothing. She looked Charlie up and down, a puzzled expression appeared on her face. "What do you want?"

"I'm here for some zombie fortune," she said, making something up on the spot.

"What? I don't understand what you're sayin'."

"I heard that with the help of a certain zrug that one lives outside their time," she explained. "Sounds similar to your services."

The woman pushed the door open wider, grabbed her arm, and pulled her in. "Fine, you come in and wait here." The woman closed and locked the door.

A couple minutes later, two men came into the living room where she waited. They looked like thugs.

"So you look a little too old," commented the first one.

"A bit too scrawny," said the second one.

She shook her head. "Look, I'm here to get drugs," she explained.

"Well, great, you're in the right place then," said the first thug. He plopped down onto a chair but didn't offer her one. The other gangster just stood there looking her over.

"So, what types of drugs do you want, and can you pay? I mean in cash. No offense, little lady," he said.

"OK, let's get one thing straight. I'm not a prostitute and I'm not for sale. I'm looking to buy."

The two men looked at each other, eyes open wide.

The first guy looked at her. "OK, we got it all. Meth, weed, though that don't sell much now seeing as you can buy it at any shop, coke, bath salts, and speed."

"We even have strychnine," said the other guy.

"What?" Charlie asked.

"You know, in case you want to off someone."

Charlie had a horrified look on her face as they laughed.

"No, I'm not trying to kill someone. I'm looking for the zombie drug. I think it's called zrug on the streets?"

The guys stopped laughing.

"Why do you want that?" asked the first guy. "That stuff is dangerous."

"Yeah, we don't deal in that," said the

second guy.

"I have money and can buy it," she explained. "Oh, and it's for a friend, not me," she added.

"Oh right, everyone buys for a friend." He put stress on the word friend.

"Right, so do you have what I want?" she asked.

"Depends," the gangster said, shifting position in his seat.

"I have the money," she said.

"It's two grand for a finger," he replied.

"A finger?" she asked. "For real?"

The guys laughed.

"That's what they call it. Not really though. Stan, go and get her stuff."

The other guy left the room muttering. "I told you not to mention my name, geez."

He came back shortly and handed a plastic baggie to her. Inside were several smaller bags.

"This looks like enough for a year," she commented.

"Just take what ya need," he said.

"OK, I think three should suffice."

"You sure? It's highly addictive."

"Not for me," she said again.

"OK, only $1,200 then."

"Fine," she said, tossing the cash on the table, getting ready to leave.

"Nice doing business with ya," they called out to her.

She left the building and headed back into the alley. She felt pleased with herself. She lifted the bag in the air and examined it.

She was nearly at the street when someone stomped up behind her and punched her in the head. She dropped to the ground.

CHAPTER 4

Charlie mentally berated herself for being so careless. She immediately rolled to the side, away from her attacker. By the time she had jumped back up, she had her dagger out.

In front of her was a zombie. Its arms were spread out. His hands reached for her. She took a step back and had a look at her surroundings. That was odd. Where did he come from?

She walked the perimeter, seeing if there were any other zombies around. As she walked, the zombie followed her around the alley. She inspected the dumpsters, but they seemed surprisingly innocent of victims. She was done and was about to turn back to the zombie when she heard a gunshot.

Charlie dropped to the ground, and then crept across the gravel to hide behind a trash can.

"It's OK," a voice called out. "I got him."

Charlie peered around the can. It was one of the drug dealers, Stan, she thought his thug friend had said. Behind him, the zombie was lying on the ground.

She came out, still clutching her dagger. "Thanks, but I had things well in hand. I was searching the alley for others."

"Obviously," he said, leering at her. "Still, can't let these bastards on the loose."

She crept closer to him. While his hair was unkempt and his clothes were wrinkled, he was relatively clean. His pupils were huge though, indicating that he had been indulging in some sort of drug or recreational pharmaceutical.

"Thanks, then. Say, why kill him? Don't your partners use them to make the zrug?"

"Yeah, of course," he said, scratching his head. "Doesn't mean that I agree with it. I'm low on the totem pole. I'd just sell weed if it were my decision."

Charlie gave a half smile. "Of course," she replied.

"Hey, you're no druggie," he commented. "So, why you here?"

"Well, the truth is that I'm a zombie slayer," she said. She wasn't sure why she shared that info, but something told her that this guy was OK, and he might have more information that she needed.

"Ah, I see!" he replied. "Still, why buy the drugs?" he frowned at her.

"What do you think?" she said, flinging her arms out, palms up.

"You a cop?" His eyelids squeezed together, noting she had no track marks on her arms.

"Nope. My quest for drugs is strictly related to finding the zombies."

"Oh. OK. You're not going to shut us down then?"

She smiled and shook her head. "I personally don't care what you do, but these zombies could infect the entire city. I can't leave one living."

"Good, I'm that way too."

"So, I'm gathering that the zrug isn't made here then?" she asked him, putting her dagger back into her back pocket.

"That's right. It's kind of hard containing these guys."

"So, any help here please? Where is the facility that makes the drugs?"

"Well, I don't really know. The plastic bags just get delivered to us."

Charlie was firm. "Is there a way you can find out?"

"I can try and see what I can find out. Come back again tomorrow night."

Charlie frowned. It appeared that she wasn't going to get any downtime or any nights off this week.

"Hey, thanks," she said, walking away.

ZZZ

"Good work, Charlie!" said Mr. George the next day after bio class. "I didn't think we'd make so much progress so quickly."

"Yes, but one thing is for certain, there are also zombies loose on the streets of Portland. I came across a few random ones already."

"Well, I think they're likely being infected by the zleader, who must be holed up somewhere nearby. So far, I've had no reports of zombies in any other parts of the city. Right now we have a one mile infection zone circumference." Stewart examined his map. "The two alleys you found zombies in are quite close together. Chances are the zleader is in hiding somewhere near there."

"Right. Well, I have to head to my next class now." She grabbed her backpack and left.

zzz

Charlie walked down the hallway to her next class.

"Hello, Mr. Allan," she called out. "That's a nice new suit you're wearing. And that's a fancy watch."

"Wow, you know your fashion," he said, waving at her. "I wouldn't have expected that of you. Zan, maybe."

Charlie headed into her chem class where Owen gave her a wave.

"I wonder how Mr. Allan found the cash to buy all that fancy stuff?" she whispered to him.

"Dunno," he said. "Maybe he got a raise."

"Curious," she said. "Say, can you do me a favor tonight? I've got to go to the bad part of town to pick something up, but I should probably have a spotter."

"Maybe," he replied. "As long as you

aren't dealing drugs."

"No, it's the opposite," she said.

"Cool, count me in!"

"Can I go too?" asked a voice.

Charlie jumped when Zan stuck her head between the two of them.

"Zan! You scared me," said Owen.

"OK, why would you head into a dangerous situation? I thought tonight you'd be chilling at home, doing your homework," asked Charlie.

"I'm getting bored. I aced all the tests this week. I already know everything."

"Hey, maybe you can skip a grade," suggested Owen.

"Already did that," Zan responded. "My parents don't want me to get too far ahead as then I won't fit in."

Charlie looked at Owen. She hated involving her friends in case they got hurt. On the other hand, she might need the help. Who knew what would happen if she went in alone, having asked for information, and they decided to lie in wait for her? The more, the merrier.

"Fine, but I'm not even going to tell you why we're going."

"Good deal," said Zan. Then she reverted

to her usual aloofness. "If you guys don't want to lend me a pen, that's fine," she said extremely loud, so the entire class heard. She stomped back to her desk at the front.

ZZZ

The group was hiding behind a large dumpster. Charlie was on the end, peering out occasionally.

"Gee, I could have done this at home too," commented Zan.

"Maybe we should call the cops," said Owen.

Charlie had given the team a bare minimum of information. She hoped that they would stay safe.

"OK, I'm going in," she said.

Fortunately, this time around, there were no zombies. She really didn't want to have to explain zombies to either of them.

She strode confidently up to the same door, with the sign FORTUNES FORETOLD situated above the entrance, and knocked.

"Hey, what's up?" asked Stan. "You ready

to buy more? Hey, let me get my jacket and I'll be right there." He grabbed his jacket, and then exited the door, closing it behind him.

"No, I don't need any more drugs," she said.

"I know, but that goon in there doesn't need to know what I'm doing," he said.

"Oh right," she said.

"Anyway, what are you doing with those drugs I sold you?"

"I turned them over to someone, and they're being sent to a lab for testing."

"I see," he said.

"So, did you learn anything?" she asked.

"Yep. Apparently John, that's the goon inside there, normally has them delivered. But they're not doing that anymore, so he has to go pick them up from The Bean Trip."

Charlie thought a bit. "You mean, the coffee shop down the street?"

He nodded.

"Is there any sort of contact?" she asked. "Or is he picking up from one of the baristas?"

"Not sure," he answered. "All I know is that John has to go there at 11 pm tonight."

"Right," she said. "Well, thanks for your time. It's greatly appreciated." She began to walk away.

"Hey, maybe the cops should handle this," he suggested.

"Yeah, like they handled the cocaine, morphine, meth, or bath salts crises."

"Well, then, stay safe!"

Charlie turned and walked back to her friends while Stan went back inside.

She walked around the dumpster. "Psst, I'm back," she said.

Owen came out first, then Zan.

"Did ya get what you want?" he asked.

"Yes, information. However, the night isn't over yet. We have to go to a coffee shop at 11 pm."

"Wait. Would it be open that late?"

"I guess so," said Charlie. "It's Portland. Does anyone sleep?"

"Great," said Owen. "We can get a bite to eat before we go there. I like this surveillance. Really hard work."

"Yeah, maybe I should have stayed home to do my math homework. That would have been more exciting," said Zan.

Charlie's arms went up in the air. "Hey, guys! Get behind me."

In the distance was a pack of zombies. There had to be at least five of them.

"Hey, those guys have too much to drink or what?" asked Owen.

"Looks like zombies to me," said Zan.

The zombies ran at them. Charlie yanked the dagger out of her back pocket. Owen looked around frantically. He spotted an old board by the dumpster so he ran and got it. Zan just stood there.

Charlie didn't wait. She raced up to the zombie on the right and smashed his head in with her dagger. Before the second zombie had a chance to reach her, he was down on the ground too.

Owen rushed forward with the board held over his head. He swung it out hard, connecting with the head of the zombie on the far left. It went down.

"Got one!" he yelled.

"You have to destroy their brains," Charlie called.

The zombie on the ground reached out a hand and clutched Owen's leg. Owen took the board and brought it down hard on the zombie's head. Blood and brains spewed everywhere. "Yuck!" he cried.

There were still two zombies walking.

"These are mine," Zan cried. She pulled something out from the inside of her jacket pocket. A second later, she plunged her dagger into their skulls. Both zombies went down.

"Geez, Zan! What are you doing?!" said Charlie, fretting.

"Quick, get them in the dumpsters," Zan said.

Five minutes later, the team of three was casually walking down the street. Owen had ditched his shirt in the first trash can he saw. He was now wearing a pink cat shirt that Zan just happened to have in her backpack.

"How do I look?" she asked. "No zombie blood anywhere?"

"Nah, you're fine," said Owen.

"Zan! I can't believe you stabbed them! I hear sirens on the way," said Charlie, complaining.

"Well, there were too many, sorry. Besides, I thought you two could use the help."

"Arrgh," said Charlie. "Let's hope the sirens don't scare away the guys from the rendezvous at The Bean Trip later."

The group walked down the street. Fortunately, the cop cars were on the next street over, so they weren't seen.

"This evening is shaping up well," said Zan. "I was right. You are a zlayer."

Charlie slapped her on the back. "And you too! I thought I was the only one in this city."

"Nah," said Zan. "We had an outbreak way south of here in Ashland a few years back. A small one though, not like this. That's when I found out."

"Cool!" said Owen. "But what's a zlayer?"

"A zombie slayer," said Charlie and Zan in unison.

"I see," he said. "Well, since we're talking about fake things, I'm a truthsayer."

Zan chuckled. "I already knew that too."

"Well, it's interesting how we all ended up together. Do any of the others at school possess superpowers?" asked Charlie.

Owen ran his fingers through his hair. "Hey, I'm a superhero!"

"Not that I'm aware of. It's not exactly something that people brag about at school," replied Zan.

"OK, guys, we're nearly there. Should we hide and wait to see who enters the shop at 11 pm? Or should we head in there first?" asked Charlie.

"I say we hide first. That worked out well last time," suggested Owen.

"OK, then. Let's duck around the alley and see who shows up."

While the three of them crouched behind the trash cans, Charlie wondered why it was easier to make friends when you were a zlayer.

CHAPTER 5

"Thanks for checking in," said Stewart. "Since you'll be in a public place, I'm not too concerned."

"See you at school tomorrow." She flipped her phone closed.

"So far, no action," said Zan, peering out at The Bean Trip across the street.

"Yep, pretty dead at night. So far, I've only seen one woman with a baby carriage, and three teenage girls. Somehow, I don't think they're our target market," said Owen.

"Shhh," said Charlie. "There's John, one of the drug dealers."

"He's going inside," said Zan.

"OK, I think we should head in," said Charlie. "Just in case the seller does work for the shop."

The three teens casually came out from behind the dumpster. Zan wiped her jeans down. They jaywalked across the street and entered the shop.

Inside, there was the distinctive aroma of coffee bean permeating the air. The coffee shop was small. There was a chalkboard up on the wall with the menu. The display case in front had a few treats.

"Hello, how may I help you?" asked the barista.

"I'd like a decaf latte with gingerbread syrup, rice milk, no whip, grande," said Zan.

"Can I just have a bottle of water?" asked Charlie, rolling her eyes.

"I'll have the veggie fruit juice," said Owen.

The group received their orders. Zan paid the bill.

They sat near the wall where they'd have a good vantage point. The drug dealer was seated on the opposite side of the wall. He hadn't even looked up when they came in. Charlie forgot she might be recognized, so she quickly put on some red lipstick and earrings from her bag, and donned a baseball cap that Zan handed to her. She untied her hair and let it rest against her shoulders. There. He shouldn't be able to recognize her now.

The woman with the baby carriage soon left, then the three teen girls, leaving only four people in the coffee shop, not including the barista.

Charlie was pretending to read her cell phone when the barista came out from behind the counter and dropped a bag on the drug dealer's table.

"I knew it!" whispered Owen.

John grabbed the bag and left the shop.

"Hey, it's almost closing time here," called out the barista.

"We're almost done, thanks," called out Charlie.

The group finished up their drinks, and then used the bathrooms. Outside, they gathered together.

"Now what?" asked Owen.

"I think I need another vocation," said Zan. "This surveillance thing is mighty boring."

"I think we should wait until the barista comes out, then jump him, and make him confess as to where he got the drugs from," suggested Charlie.

"What?" said Owen. "That's crazy. That's like committing a crime. I'm out." He walked away.

"Owen!" called Zan.

"Crap!" said Charlie. "I need help with this."

"I'll help you. I can make him talk." Zan had a smirk on her face.

"OK, but I need to let Stewart know first." She grabbed her phone out of her pocket.

"Wait a minute, Stewart? As in Stewart George? You got a thing going on with him or something? He's old!"

"No!" Charlie said, horrified. "He's my mentor."

"Oh, I see," said Zan.

"Speaking of mentors, who's yours?" asked Charlie.

"Mine? She got killed a couple years ago, during the last uprising."

"So, you've been going it alone?"

"Yeah, well, nothing's happened since then. And no one has showed up."

"That's crazy," said Charlie.

They both ducked into the same alley, waiting for the worker to finish closing up the shop.

Finally, he exited the building and locked the door. He'd forgotten to take his apron off, but he had his backpack on his back.

Charlie and Zan raced across the street, getting honked at by a car that was going a bit too fast. The barista looked up at them, not thinking anything was amiss. Zan rushed forward, grabbing the back of his jacket and his arm. Charlie took his other arm. They pulled him back to the entrance of the coffee shop. At least there was a small alcove where they should have minimal privacy, though it was pretty quiet at night, and nothing much was happening.

"Hey! What's up?" cried the guy.

"You're going to tell us where you got the drugs," said Zan.

"What are you talking about?" he cried out.

"Hey, Z. Let me handle this," said Charlie.

Zan nodded.

"OK, you're going to tell us where you got the drugs," said Charlie.

"What drugs?" the guy asked obliviously.

"The ones you gave John, the drug dealer, in the coffee shop," said Charlie.

Zan was shaking the guy back and forth and wouldn't let him go.

"The zrugs," clarified Charlie.

"OK, OK, you got me," he said. "Yes, I

sold zrugs to John."

"Good," said Zan. "Where did you get them from?"

"Nowhere," said the guy. "We make them here at the coffee shop."

"Really?" asked Charlie. This was fantastic! Her work was nearly done. Find the source of the zombies and then she could go back to retirement.

"Yep," he said. "We make it in the back. There's a tiny storeroom beside the bathrooms you may not have noticed. Say, what are you going to do with me?"

"We'll beat you up unless you tell us everything," said Zan.

Charlie pushed her off of him. "No, we won't."

"Say, if I give you some zrugs, will you let me go? We've got some stored in the back here."

"No," said Charlie. "We're not actually after the zrugs."

"No?" asked the guy, relieved.

"We actually need to know where you got the zombies to make the drugs."

"Oh, is that all?" he said. "We've got one in the back."

"What the?" exclaimed Zan, grabbing his

arm again.

"Easy," said Charlie, trying to block her from grabbing him again.

"Yep, in the back."

"Is it alive? Errr, you know what I mean," asked Charlie.

"Yep," said the guy. "You can come have a look if you want." He took out his keys and unlocked the door. He opened it, and the group walked inside. He flicked on the light switch to reveal the coffee shop.

"Where do we go?" asked Zan.

"This way," he said. He headed to the back where the bathrooms were located. Beside the two bathrooms was another door with a deadbolt on it.

"My name is Steve, by the way. I'm the barista at the shop here. I'm just trying to get some work experience under my belt and save some cash. I desperately want to get outta this dead end. Unfortunately, that means roommates, so I have to deal with Stan and John a little while longer until I can get my own place."

"You're quite the chatterbox, aren't you?" Zan said.

"Hey, Steve. Anyway…" Charlie shot a dirty look at Zan. "I'm Chi and this is Z," said Charlie, not wanting to give him their real names.

Steve found the proper key and opened up the door. When it opened, there was a terrible reek from inside. The girls immediately covered their faces.

Steve flicked on the light. The room was quite large, considering it was only a storeroom. "This used to be our back room for events, but the owner decided he wanted to sell drugs instead."

"Geez, Steve. Couldn't you have found another job?" asked Zan.

He shrugged. "I don't know. Again, I'm trying to work my way up, making something of my life. Right now I live with two other drug dealers, John, who I give the drugs to, and Stan, who isn't such a bad guy, but like I said before, I wanna get out of this dead end place. And it helps that they pay me $30 an hour to keep my mouth shut."

"Wow," said Charlie, impressed. "Do you think I can get a job here?"

He shrugged, and led them into the back. At the very back was what appeared to be a body bag in the shape of a human. It was attached firmly to the wall. Every now and then the bag rippled.

"I can't believe you'd keep a human being in here," said Charlie. "Not only is this ethically unacceptable, but it's illegal too."

Zan smiled. "You tell him!"

"Take a chill pill," Steve said. "We don't always have one here. This one arrived this morning."

"So, some guy brings you zombies, and then you extract the blood from their brains to make the drugs?" asked Charlie.

"Something like that," said Steve.

They watched as Zan unzipped the bag. She pulled the fabric apart. Inside, there was a man, considerably decayed. He tried to lean forward to bite her, but his mouth was duct-taped shut.

"Say, if he's completely dead, can you still extract the chemicals from his brain?" asked Zan.

"Well, no," said Steve. "He has to be alive for them to be useful." Steve looked at Charlie. Then her eyes widened.

"Zan, no!" she cried.

Steve turned to watch as Zan lifted her dagger and plunged it into the zombie's eye socket. The zombie was soon a hundred percent dead.

"Hey!" cried Steve. "How am I going to

explain that to my boss?"

Charlie grabbed Steve's arm and pulled him from the room. She made him sit down at one of the tables.

"Steve, where does your boss get the zombies from?" she asked.

He had his hands over his face. "Umm, some weird lady comes in with them on a regular basis. One every three days."

"Weird lady?" asked Charlie.

"Yeah. She has these weird green glowing eyes. Fancy contact lenses, I guess. But sometimes she'd come in without them on too."

"Steve, I love ya!" she said, patting him on the back. Then she sniffed the air. "What the?"

Zan came running out of the back. "Run! The shop is on fire!"

The group raced from the coffee shop and ran across the street. A loud explosion was heard from inside the shop. The entire building went up in flames. The windows burst and loud explosions were heard as the flames hit the gas pipes.

"Thanks, guys!" said Steve, running down the street. "You've saved me from working for that gang owner." He actually seemed happy. He hummed aloud as he headed for his car.

Charlie was furious. She punched Zan on the shoulder. "Why did you do that?" she screamed at her.

"Relax. We could never have had enough time to search that place. This way, the evidence of zombies is gone, all the drugs are gone, the lab equipment, the formulas. And Steve can lead a happy and fulfilling life."

"Yeah, except that we still need to find the zleader," said Charlie.

"Well, one step at a time," said Zan.

"You know what," said Charlie. "I don't need your help anymore. I'm done." She turned and walked away.

zzz

"I'm really angry at you," said Stewart. They were in her backyard, far away from the house, so that Gran wasn't woken up.

"It's not my fault! She's crazy," said Charlie.

"She was your responsibility. And I

thought that you wanted to work alone."

"I know," she said. "I'm sorry. What a mess."

"And what happened to Owen?"

"Right. He didn't want to get involved and took off."

"And you should have gone with him," said Stewart. "Well, the one benefit is that we've put a stop to their drug operation. I'm just really disappointed that we missed out on the further opportunity of finding the zleader though."

"OK, what's the next step then? It took me a long time to get this far, and it's led nowhere."

Stewart paced the yard. "I'll have to see if there have been any more sightings."

"Maybe I can go back to the area tomorrow and check out the rest of the businesses, maybe some of the apartments. I think I can gain access to that building with the broken window, unless they've fixed it. I'll bet she's holed up there."

"Well, before you do that, let me make some calls first. And I'd be surprised if she sticks around after the fire. She may realize that someone deliberately torched the place."

"Well, either that or making drugs is dangerous. Could have been related to that," she suggested.

"Yes, I expect that's what the police report will say. We will have to see. I'm still not certain how much brainpower a zleader really has. Usually their one goal is power, and to control not only the human population, but the zombie population as well."

"Same thing," said Charlie.

They both had a good chuckle over that.

"Well, I supposed I should get at least a few hours of sleep tonight. I hope you aren't still mad at me."

"No. I'll have a chat with Zan. We don't need anyone interfering in our project."

CHAPTER 6

The next week was fairly uneventful for
Charlie. She had decided to focus on her
schoolwork. While Owen remained friendly,
he didn't want to hang out with her. Zan
wanted to hang out, but she declined. She
didn't know how the meeting had gone
between Zan and Stewart, but she didn't
care.

It seemed fairly quiet in the city. There
hadn't been any more sightings of zombies.

Charlie felt that it was all a well-deserved
rest. Perhaps this was the end of it. Maybe
the zleader would go away and she wouldn't
be required to do anything more.

ZZZ

It was almost too quiet, and while Charlie enjoyed the peace and quiet, she wondered if any progress had been made. She decided to send Stewart a text.

"Any news about the zleader?" she typed. She pressed send.

The answer came back quickly. "None. Maybe someone else did our job."

"Keep me posted," she typed.

"CU in class," he responded.

She headed off to her philosophy class.

"Students, next weekend is our annual camping trip. I hope everyone will sign up. It's going to be a collaborative type of experience. We'll leave early on Friday morning, and come back on Sunday night. This is a great time to learn about the great outdoors and become a community."

Charlie rolled her eyes. Of course, she was in camping world.

The teacher handed out the signup forms.

Owen sat beside her, enthusiastically filling out the forms. "Psst," he said to her. "You going?"

"Yeah, sure. Why not?" she replied.

Class finished and they both hung behind.

"Hey, I'm sorry for abandoning you the other day. I heard about the fire. What on earth happened?"

"First of all, don't worry about leaving. I would have done the same thing if I could've," she replied. She placed her books back into her bag. She glanced up to make sure that the teacher and the other students had left the classroom. "It was crazy. Zan just took charge and did her own thing," she explained.

"Man, that's crazy. I see that you two aren't talking to each other," he said.

"I'm still furious with her. And Stewart, err, Mr. George was mad at us too. She set fire to the coffee shop to destroy the zombie and the zrugs, not thinking that was only half of our case."

"Geez," he said.

"Now all trails have gone dry for finding the zleader, which was our goal in the first place," she added.

"That's a drag," he said. "But I don't think I could have stopped any of that, even if I had stayed."

She smiled and nodded.

"I'm looking forward to this upcoming camping trip next weekend. Should be fun," Owen commented.

"I think it's stupid, but it'll be good to

have a rest. Interact with nature, instead of horrific creatures," she said.

"Oh, but you haven't seen squirrels. You really have to watch those guys." They both had a good laugh about that.

zzz

The school buses loaded up with students. This trip involved about one hundred 11th grade students, so a fair chunk of the school. Principal Allan oversaw the loading of the buses. He seemed quite pleased with himself.

"We've never had such high attendance for our camping expedition before," he bragged to Zan. She just rolled her eyes.

"Some of us were told by our parents to go," she commented.

"Grrr!" commented Charlie. "I can't believe she's going!"

"Cool down," said Owen. "Just ignore her. What could possibly go wrong on a camping trip?"

"Right. After all, the zombies are in the city, not in the country, right?"

He nodded.

"Actually, that's a fact. In my entire history of zombie slaying, zombies are always skulking around in the busiest sections of the city. They like to have a ready food source."

Owen nodded. "That's comforting to know."

"Say, have you been practicing your self-defense skills?" she asked.

He nodded. "Yep. I got some DVDs and everything."

"Good," she said. "Because there's a class in the early afternoon."

He nodded. "I'll be there."

The trip to the campsite took a short length of time. It was near Multnomah Falls. Charlie wished she'd been able to bring her own car, but there were rules.

The students hopped out of the bus, collecting their gear from the stowage compartment at the back of the vehicle.

"This way," called Principal Allan. "We'll get everyone settled in at the campsite before we start our classes."

"Groan," said Zan. "Can't even get away from them on the weekend."

"Good, then you won't be in mine,"

Charlie said to her.

Zan just walked away.

Charlie and Owen headed up to the campsite. There were several small tents set up close to each other.

"Cool," said Charlie. In the distance, she could hear Zan groaning.

"Hey, maybe we can share a tent?" said Owen.

Charlie laughed.

"What a drag," said Owen. "You're right. They won't let us."

Charlie was relieved when she didn't have to share a tent, because there were an odd number of girls. She didn't know where Zan was, and she didn't care.

Her tent was situated in the middle of the clearing, beside Owen and Mike's tent. Mike was one of the other 11th grade students, but she hadn't really had an opportunity to say much to him.

"Hey, Charlie. This is Mike," said Owen.

"Hi, Mike. Nice to meet you," she said, shaking his hand.

"Mike is looking after his mom. She has cancer."

"Oh, that is wonderful of you," said Charlie.

"Thanks," said Mike. "I'm looking forward to graduation this year. Then I'll have some extra time with her. It's only a matter of time," he commented.

"Who's looking after her while you're here?" asked Charlie.

"My sister. She's 16. She can manage for a day or two."

Charlie and Owen smiled at him.

"OK, so, where's the food?" asked Charlie. "I'm hungry."

The group found the cabin with the dining hall in it. The food was fairly basic, salads, mac and cheese, and hot dogs, but it filled them up.

ZZZ

It was early afternoon when several students met near the bonfire site to participate in a self-defense class. After ten minutes, the teacher was a no-show.

"That's odd," said Charlie.

"Maybe we should just start without him?" suggested Owen.

She smiled. "Listen up, class. I've had

martial arts training. I can show you some basic self-defense moves until, or if, the teacher arrives."

Some of the students looked disappointed, hoping that this would be a free period instead.

After a few minutes, Charlie was getting frustrated. She should give a lot more credit to teachers. How did they do it? Here were ten students. Half of them didn't even want to be here. The other half did, but of these, most of them had trouble following basic instructions about defensive moves.

"OK, whoever doesn't want to be here, get out. You're wasting my time," she yelled.

"But, we need our card stamped for the credit," protested a guy in the back.

"Then go bother another class," she said. She was pleased when half the students left. That left just the five, plus her. That included Owen and Mike, who were doing surprisingly well.

"OK, so a zombie is coming up at you from the front. Let's pretend you have a sharp object in your right hand, or left, if you're left-handed. Raise your arm to a level with their eye socket. Then take the dagger and plunge it right in," she recommended.

"Excuse me?" asked Mike. "Zombies?"

"Yes, we're going to have some fun with this," she said. "In the event there is a zombie uprising, then we must be prepared."

Owen raised his hand. "But, what about if we're attacked by humans? We wouldn't use as much violence," he said.

"True," she said. "But we'll get to that next. First things first."

She spent the next half an hour telling them how to defend themselves against zombies. Then she covered attacks by humans, which was a whole lot simpler. When she got their scorecards back, she saw that everyone had given her a ten out of ten.

Their next class was on knot tying, which was somewhat interesting. Charlie thought it would be good to know how to tie up zombies. Everyone took it in good humor.

It was now time for dinner, so she headed for the dining hall.

It was the same food as lunch, so she chose mac and cheese instead of hot dogs. She really hoped there would be something different the next day.

"How is everyone doing?" asked Owen.

"Good," everyone said through

mouthfuls of food.

"I heard there's a nature walk tonight," said Mike. "We get to bring our flashlights and walk in the dark."

"Sounds like fun," said Owen.

"Great," said Charlie. "Sounds like I'll have to tag along so no one does anything stupid."

"I heard that there's going to be a party at the dining hall for those who stay behind," said Mike.

"Hmm, tempting," said Charlie. "But I'd better go with them. What are the teachers thinking, allowing inexperienced students to traipse around in the dark? There could be coyotes, bears, and cougars out there."

"Oh my!" said Owen.

Everyone laughed.

"Ahhhh!" screamed one of the students in the distance.

"What the?" called out Mike.

"She bit me!" cried a student.

"What?" shouted Charlie. She jumped out of her chair and raced to the other table.

A student held up her arm. There was a distinctive human teeth-shaped wound near the elbow. "Why did you do that?" she yelled at her friend.

"I don't know," said the girl. "Something came over me."

Charlie rushed over to her and looked in her eyes. They seemed normal. She wasn't drooling. She reached out a hand to touch her face. It did seem a bit warm.

"I think both need to be sent to First Aid," she said, as Principal Allan walked up. "There's an incidence of typhoid fever in the city. She may have given it to the other student. Both need medical assistance," Charlie explained.

Principal Allan frowned at her but agreed. Both students were escorted to the First-Aid building.

"Oh, and lock them in," she said. "We don't want the fever to spread."

Principal Allan looked like he wanted to ask her questions, but he had to get the students to First Aid.

After they left, she and Owen whispered to each other.

"Man, I don't like that," said Owen. "Was that a zombie?"

"It's curious," she replied. "Usually, their eyes glow green and they display more symptoms. What are their names?" she asked.

Owen replied, "That was Tonia who bit Sam."

"The trouble with zombie outbreaks is that they're ever evolving and changing. I guess we'll have the answer in a couple of hours if they both start turning."

"Yep," said Owen. "Perhaps we should just cancel tonight's walk?"

"Nah, it's in an hour, and only half an hour long. If they turn, it won't be for another two or three hours. We have plenty of time. I can make sure everyone stays safe on the nature walk, then get back here in time to check on Tonia and Sam."

"We might have to sleep outside tonight to watch them," suggested Owen.

"Yeah, that's the spirit!"

"OK, I'm going to go brush my teeth, then I'll meet you at the beach for the start of the walk," said Owen.

"That sounds like a plan," she replied. "It's odd, but I can't help but feel that I'm missing something here. Well, let's hope that I figure it out over the next couple of hours."

Owen nodded. He headed off to his tent, while Charlie headed to hers. She wanted to grab her pair of hiking boots. It would help to carry one of her daggers. She hoped that Principal Allan didn't figure it out. It would be disastrous if she had her weapons taken away from her, especially if something bad did happen.

She tucked one of them in her back pants pocket, complete with protective pouch so that she didn't accidentally stab herself sitting down.

CHAPTER 7

The nature walk began at the lake. Charlie purposefully was the last in line. Owen was just ahead of her. In front were two teachers that she didn't know. They were probably from arts or cooking classes that she felt were useless.

"I don't like this," said Owen. "What was up back there?"

"I'm not certain. I'd hate to jump the gun and call Stewart, err, Mr. George though."

"Hmm. Maybe you should. You're supposed to check in after all."

"Right. Well, there's nothing to do on this boring walk anyway." She hung back a bit more, but made certain that she could see Owen ahead of her. At regular intervals, he'd look back to check on her.

"Hey, what's up?" asked Stewart. "I was just getting dinner."

She sighed. "Well, I'm not certain it's anything, really."

"Oh? How is camping?" he asked.

"Quite honestly, really, really boring. I had to inject some zombie humor into my self-defense class, otherwise, everyone would have fallen asleep." As she walked down the dirt pathway, she reached out an arm to brush against the shrubs that framed the path.

"You what?" he said, trying to control his voice.

"Don't worry, I didn't tell them the truth. I just gave them tips in case there was a zombie apocalypse."

"What did I say about keeping a low profile? You could have mentioned vampires instead. Why zombies? You need to stick to fictitious things that aren't real."

"I know, right. I'll be more careful next time. Trouble is that I was in a class with my truthsayer friend."

"Darn it," said Stewart. "Maybe you should stay away from him. What are you going to do if you let something slip when you find the zleader?"

"Well, I was trying to practice keeping my mouth shut, and it's worked pretty good so far. I guess if I stop being creative and focus, then that will help me a lot."

"Good, good," he said. "So, why did you really call me?"

Charlie sighed. If he was unhappy with her joking about zombies, then he was going to be unhappy to hear this.

"OK, so, at dinner tonight, one of the students bit another," she started to explain.

"Oh my god, what?" he exclaimed.

"It was a little bite, barely broke the skin. But I suggested to Principal Allan that both be confined to the first-aid room, as it might be typhoid fever. He didn't object."

"Typhoid, you're funny!" he said. "So, did either of them exhibit zombie tendencies?" he asked.

"Actually, no," she replied. "Tonia bit Sam. When they were escorted away, they both seemed fine. Tonia was apologetic. She didn't have glowing green eyes or anything."

There was silence on the other end.

And then, something that sounded like a storm came out from the other end of the telephone. Charlie had to hold it far away from her head. There was a long stream of extremely bad words she'd heard before but would get in trouble if she said them in front of Gran.

When the harangue ended, she asked, "So, what's up?"

"Don't you get it?" he said into the telephone.

"Mmmm?"

"A zombie who doesn't look like a zombie? One who probably is wearing contact lenses?"

"What? Are you certain?" she asked. "How is that even possible?"

"You'll have to track her down and kill her."

"But, I don't have my special dagger yet!"

"Damn it, you're right! I'll have to drive out there tonight and meet you. OK. Here's the plan. Do not engage with her. Continue on with whatever you're doing right now."

"Got it," she said. "I'll just continue on this nature walk we're doing."

"Good, I'll text you when I'm there, and we can arrange to meet for the exchange of the dagger."

"Ooh," she squealed. "It's ready then?"

"Yep, it's ready. Gotta go." He hung up.

Owen looked concerned. "So, what was that about?"

"Apparently Tonia could be the zleader!

Who knew?"

"I meant to ask you earlier, but what on earth is a zleader?" he asked.

By now, both of them were far away from the group ahead. They weren't concerned about being overheard.

"Well, apparently when the first zleader or zombie leader dies, the person they most recently bit becomes the new zleader. There can be benefits. If they are too far-gone, they actually regenerate skin, bones, and hair. They start looking as human as you and me. Usually, they leave the city they're in, and they move to a new city."

"Why?" he asked.

"You know, we're not really sure. We think it might have something to do with respect for the last dead zleader or something."

"So, if every city had a zleader, and they were killed, there would be none left to make new zombies?"

She nodded. "Well, technically. Obviously we don't want a zleader in every town. Can you imagine the chaos? It would be the end of the world."

Just then, they heard rustling sounds coming from ahead.

"Did you miss me?" asked Zan. "It sounds like you need me if the zleader is close."

"Dammit, were you listening in again?" said Charlie.

"Of course. It's my job," Zan said, smirking.

"Fine, but from now on, you follow my orders. It's your fault that we're even here," Charlie said, berating her.

"Yeah, it's my fault we're camping." She paused. "Well, actually it's my parents' fault. They wanted me to go."

"OK, great. Make up already," said Owen. "We should catch up with the others. Otherwise, they'll wonder where we are."

"Let's go," said Zan.

"Fine," said Charlie, grabbing her hand.

"Hey," said Zan. "Too close!"

Owen rolled his eyes.

"Say, you came back," Zan said to him.

"Yep, well, I'm the wuss in the group. You ladies tackle the rough stuff. I'll tackle the mind hacking."

"You can do mind hacking?" she asked. "Hmmm."

Just then, there was a commotion from up ahead. The screaming started moments later.

"And so it begins," said Charlie.

ZZZ

Charlie, Owen, and Zan raced down the path to find the other students. When they arrived, there were four lying in the path, trying to get up. The rest of the students had scattered, except for one who was chowing down on the teacher on the far end of the path.

"What happened?" cried Owen.

"Someone went crazy," said one of the students lying on the ground. Owen helped him to stand up.

"You weren't bitten, were you?" he asked.

"Nope, don't think so, but that guy wasn't so lucky." He nodded at the student eating the teacher. By now, blood and guts were everywhere. Fortunately, the teacher was already dead.

Charlie tiptoed up to the student. It wasn't anyone she knew. He was probably from the art or the cooking classes. She pulled the dagger from her back pocket and quickly plunged it into the student's head. He went down fast.

She walked another step and did the same to the teacher. She wasn't taking any chances, even though when humans were too far eaten they often didn't turn into zombies themselves.

"Man, that's crazy," said Owen. "Are there zombies everywhere now?"

Charlie shook her head.

Zan was running around the path, checking the other students. She'd already dispatched one of the students who had glowing green eyes. Fortunately, the other students outside their group didn't see her do it.

"What a mess. We need to find some adults in charge," said Owen.

"Good luck with that," said Charlie. "Where did the others go?"

"They scattered as soon as the attack happened. That zombie guy came at us and pushed us down. Oh crap," the other guy said, as he saw that one of the other students hadn't made it.

"What's your name?" asked Charlie.

"Ben," he replied.

"Ben, I'm Charlie. That's Zan and Owen.

Can you help us find the other students? If any one of them has been bitten, they can turn into zombies too."

He nodded, and followed them down the path.

They walked for a bit, but Charlie had the sneaking feeling that the students had scattered into the forest and weren't even on the path anymore.

"Hey, I think we're going to have to report this. How can we expect to hunt for zombies if we're in the middle of the forest?" said Zan.

"Good point," said Charlie. "Maybe we can be the bait? You have a dagger, right?"

Zan nodded.

Owen came striding up. "I have this," he said, holding up a sharp stick.

Charlie rolled her eyes. "Just make sure that you aim for the eye socket with that, otherwise, it'll be useless."

He grinned.

"I have an idea," she added. "Let's draw them to us now."

"OK, but I have a question," said Owen, sticking his head close to her. "That student had to have been bitten by someone else first. So, where did that zombie go?"

"Good question," she said. "Let's do this and see if we can draw them out. There is at least one other zombie out there."

"OK, let's do it," said Zan.

Everyone gathered up what sticks and rocks they could carry. Once they had what they needed, they gathered together on the path.

"OK, one, two, three," cried out Charlie.

"Ahhhhhh," yelled the team in unison. They used the sticks against the bushes and shrubs to make noise. They banged rocks together.

After a couple minutes, there was success. The bushes in front of them moved. Charlie held up her arm for them to hush. Then there was silence. But the noise still came from the bushes. Out walked one of the other teachers. Her eyes glowed green. Her nose had decayed and was rotting the flesh off her face while her lips had fallen away from her jawline, exposing a row of teeth.

Zan rushed up and killed her with the dagger in her hand.

Charlie looked around but didn't see anyone else. By now, they were almost back at the beach, as the path took a circuitous route. The group entered the clearing.

There were a bunch of students on the beach. Some looked on edge while others were happy to see them.

"Ben," said Charlie. "I need you to take attendance. We need to know anyone who is missing."

"Will do," he said, pulling out his smartphone.

"I'll check the others and make sure no one else has been bitten," said Zan, rushing away.

"Good idea," said Charlie. She walked up to the lake and washed her dagger off, then placed it back in the holster in her back pocket.

Ben came rushing up to her. "If we include those who were killed, then I think everyone is accounted for, except for Tonia and Sam."

"Great," she said. "And except for whoever bit the first person."

"Probably someone ran in and bit them, and then ran off," said Owen, trying to be helpful.

"Yep, that's my best guess. I suggest people stay here, as it's a wide-open space and you can see danger coming. Also, people need to gather together weapons,"

Charlie instructed Ben. "While you do that, Owen, Zan, and I will head to the campsite and see what's up."

She headed in that direction, with Owen and Zan following.

"Say, weren't you supposed to check on Tonia and Sam?" asked Owen.

"That's right," she said. "Probably shouldn't have listened to Stewart and just done it right away. My best guess is that Tonia and Sam are on the loose now."

"Darn it," said Zan. "We should have snuck out when we could've and offed them right away."

"Yeah, but there were just too many people watching. As it is, how do we explain what happened on the path? Even the zombies are dead. Perhaps we should have chained one of them up. What a mess," she commented.

"Well, I don't think that's going to be an issue," said Zan. "Things are escalating here. There may be no one left alive to explain to the cops what happened."

"I hope not. Otherwise, we haven't done our jobs properly," said Charlie. "Say, Owen, if you're near a person, can you detect if they're a zombie or not?"

"Yeah, but we already know when they're zombies. Their eyes glow green and they want to eat human flesh."

"I mean in finding the zleader, who obviously knows how to mask her appearance."

"Yes. Yes, I can," he said.

CHAPTER 8

Owen, Zan, and Charlie headed to the campsite where the tents were set up, while Ben remained behind.

"Say, I wonder where my roommate is?" asked Owen.

"You mean Mike?" asked Zan. "I haven't seen him around here anywhere."

As they entered the clearing, they saw the camp in disarray. Some tents had been collapsed, with camping gear strewn everywhere.

"Hey, guys! Where have you been?" called out a voice behind them.

"Mike! I was wondering where you were!" said Owen.

"I'm fine. I just had to stay behind to look after the camp."

Zan looked around her. "Wow, good job!"

"No," he said in protest. "The camp was fine until Principal Allan came along," explained Mike.

Charlie wandered around, tidying things up. "Oh crap. We'd better get this straightened up before the teachers find out. This day has been a total mess!"

"Wait, it was Principal Allan who messed up the campsite?" Zan asked.

"Yep," said Mike. "He was tearing through the site, looking for zombies."

"Zombies?" asked Charlie. "So, he knows they're a thing. That means there's another problem on site."

"Did he find any?" asked Owen.

"No," said Mike.

"OK, you guys stay here. I'm going to go check on where they put Sam and Tonia. I'm guessing they got out, or something."

"Wait, I'm coming with you," said Zan.

"OK, Owen and Mike, get this camp back in order," instructed Charlie.

"On it," said Mike.

"I'm going to haul this load to the school bus," said Owen.

Zan followed after Charlie. "I wonder where Allan is?"

"Don't know, but let's get this checked

out," said Charlie.

The first-aid cabin was up ahead. The two girls quietly snuck up to it. The door was closed. Charlie went up to one window, motioning Zan to check out the other window.

"I can't see anything," she whispered back at her.

"That's because it's empty," Charlie whispered back, wondering why they were being so quiet when there wasn't anyone inside.

Charlie walked up to the door and opened it. "Nope, no one here. It appears that nothing has been touched."

"That means they didn't make it back here," Zan said.

"Nope."

Charlie closed the door and then looked around. "Stewart can't get here fast enough with that dagger."

"Any chance he can speed it up?" asked Zan.

"I'll try," she said, pulling her cell phone from her pocket. "Don't go far," she commanded, as she watched Zan wandering around.

"No signal. Darn it! I'll have to go back to

the beach." She put her phone back in her pocket.

"Yuck!" yelled Zan. Charlie raced over to the bushes where she was standing.

Sam was on the ground, almost completely disemboweled. Zan took out her dagger and ran it through her head. "There. Should we be getting rid of the bodies?" she asked.

"Let's just tuck them into the bushes for now so no one else is alarmed," said Charlie. "When and if the police arrive, they'll find them and deal with them then. Should have done this with the others. It would keep the civilians from panicking and freaking out, at least for a short time."

"OK, so, Tonia is actually a zombie. But she must still be hungry because she ate her victim instead of biting and turning her."

"Right," said Charlie. "That might mean that there aren't too many others out here."

"Help! Help! Help!" yelled a voice in the distance.

The girls raced away from the first-aid building and back to the campsite. It had been considerably tidied up. But right in the middle, there was a girl on top of Mike. She was biting his neck.

"Hey, you sure that's a zombie and not a vampire?" asked Zan.

"No such thing as vampires," said Charlie, running in.

Both Zan and Charlie plunged their daggers into the zombie girl's head, to little effect. She merely let go of Mike's throat. Mike was already gone.

The girl peered into Charlie's eyes. One of her eyes glowed green, a colored contact lens sticking out of the corner. The other eye was a normal blue color.

"Give it up," the zombie girl said. "Soon, the world will be mine!"

"Don't think so," said Charlie, tossing her backpack on the ground and pulling out a larger blade. She swung it wide. It connected with flesh, muscle, and bone. Tonia's head lulled forward, only connected by a bit of gristle and tendons.

Charlie went in for one more cut, but right before her eyes she watched as the girl regenerated her muscles and bones. It took seconds. Her head was back where it should be.

"Whoa!" said Zan. "I knew that could happen but never seen it in person before."

Charlie smiled. "It is rather amazing, isn't

it? However, we have a problem."

Zan ran forward and quickly dispatched Mike before he could turn. "Sorry, Mike," she said.

"Damn," said Charlie. "That guy had a sick mom and a sister."

"Everyone's family is messed up," said Zan, warily watching Tonia.

"So, you are Tonia?" asked Charlie.

"Yesssss," the zombie leader said. Since her body had to momentarily regenerate itself, she had slowed down considerably. She didn't even notice as Zan pulled rope out of her backpack and tied her to the nearest tree.

"Smart," said Charlie. "I didn't think of that. You should be on my team."

"I am on your team," Zan said. The girls smiled at each other.

"OK, I'm going to hide this guy." Zan pulled the body behind the bushes.

Behind them were some stomping sounds. A man rushed into the clearing. "Oh thank god, you girls are all right." It was Principal Allan.

"Well, we are, but Mike and Sam didn't make it," explained Charlie.

"That's sad," the Principal said. "I've put

most of the students onto the bus and they are on the way out of here. I did have the sense to check them for cuts and bites before they departed, as the last thing we need is for them to turn and infect the city."

"Great," said Charlie. "Say, was Ben on that bus?"

"Yes, he was."

"Good. That's something anyway."

"So, I counted all of the students on the bus plus the remaining teachers," said the principal.

"OK, so that leaves me, Zan, Owen—wait, was Owen on the bus?"

"No, he chose to stay behind," said Allan.

"What about camp personnel?" asked Zan.

"They're fine. I've instructed them to go home," said Allan.

"Isn't it a bit odd that there are so many people here and yet no one is batting an eye that zombies are real?" asked Charlie.

"Well, this is Oregon after all," said Zan.

"Yes, I know what zombies are, thanks. And yes, this is Oregon where creatures naturally like to congregate. Oh, nice job by the way of subduing the zleader. However, her strength will soon improve and she'll be too strong for those bonds," said Principal Allan.

"How do you know——?" Charlie asked.

"Not now. I'll explain later," Allan replied.

Zan went over and tied more rope around her body. "This should give us another hour."

"So, what's next then?" asked Charlie.

"Say, where is Owen? He really shouldn't be wandering around outside by himself. I know he's growing more confident in his fighting, but he still doesn't have our experience."

"I'd send him a text, but my phone isn't working," explained Charlie.

"That's odd," said Zan. "My phone was working here earlier when we set up camp."

Principal Allan checked his phone, but he couldn't get a signal either.

"Oh, thank god! There you are! I didn't think I would find you guys!" said Owen, entering the clearing.

"We were just about to send out a posse to find you," said Charlie.

"Well, I could have just gone back to the city, but I decided to find you guys instead."

"Right. What's next?" asked Charlie.

"Ahhh!" screamed Zan. "Get her off me!" She was fighting Tonia. Tonia rushed in and bit Zan on the shoulder. She must have escaped the ropes. Zan punched her in the face. Tonia backed off, and then went barreling into Principal Allan, Charlie, and Owen. They tried to block her, but she knocked them over and raced away.

"Dammit!" said Charlie. "We should have been watching better."

"Quick! Let's get her to my car. I have an anti-serum that will at least slow down the process." They propped Zan up and began the trek to Allan's vehicle.

"I think once we get this done, we should head back to the city," said Principal Allan.

"But what about Tonia?" asked Charlie. "Shouldn't we go after her first? Or the other student or zombie?"

"Tonia isn't going to make the mistake of hanging around here, especially when she knows we're out to hunt her. I think she's heading back to Portland," explained Principal Allan.

"That's great," said Charlie. "But I need to reach Stewart, as he has something I need." She tried to call him again, but the phone still had no reception.

The group raced back to Principal Allan's car. He used his fob to unlock it, and then opened up the trunk. Inside was a sizeable first-aid kit. He quickly popped the latch to open it up. What looked like a vaccine bottle was off to the side. He quickly grabbed a syringe and the bottle. He unwrapped the syringe, flicked off the plastic cap, and inserted it into the bottle.

While he was doing that, Owen leaned Zan up against the side of the car while Charlie opened the doors of the car and got it started up.

"How do you feel?" asked Owen.

"Brain dead," said Zan. "So, this is what it feels like. And darn it, the bite is so close to my head. If she had bitten my hand, I would have just chopped it off."

"Don't worry. Allan has something to slow down the process," he said, rolling up her sleeve.

"OK, folks, hold her down. This is going to hurt a bit," he said. Owen held the zombie slayer down.

Principal Allan held the large syringe in his hand. He plunged it down into her left shoulder.

"Arrghh," Zan cried, trying not to scream.

"OK, that's done." Principal Allan put the cap back on the syringe and put it into a disposables box inside his vehicle.

Owen pulled her sleeve back down again. "So, what does that actually do?"

"It stops the zombie virus from reaching her brain," said Principal Allan.

"For how long?" asked Charlie from the interior of the vehicle.

Principal Allan sighed, and then paused. "Quite honestly, it's only a temporary fix until we can get her to her family to say goodbye."

A tear ran down Zan's face. This was the first time anyone had seen vulnerability in her.

"OK, let's go," said Allan.

Charlie quickly looked at her phone again, waiting for the others to get in the vehicle. "Hey, I have service," she said.

"Don't come," she texted Stewart. "Z disaster at camp. We're coming back to the city."

"OK," he texted back. "But city is quarantined. No one in or out. Outbreak."

"Damn!" she said. "Bad news. We can't get back into the city. It's closed off due to an outbreak."

"Will try to get the dagger to you somehow," Stewart texted again.

By now everyone was in the car and buckled up. Charlie pulled the car out of the parking lot.

"Say," Principal Allan started to speak. "There might be another idea."

"What is it?" Owen asked, as he checked the wound on Zan's shoulder. It actually appeared to be healing over.

"Well, I'm not an expert, but there are other outcomes besides her dying," he said.

"Oh, you mean letting her turn?" asked Charlie.

CHAPTER 9

The group was in the car, driving as close as they could to Portland. Charlie drove the vehicle, with Principal Allan in the passenger seat. Owen sat in the back seat with Zan, who appeared to be slowly turning.

"Pee yew!" said Owen. "Something in the vehicle smells."

"Well, that's normal," said Allan.

"Hey, her eyes are turning green. Is that normal, even with the vaccine?" asked Charlie, keeping an eye on Zan in the rearview mirror.

"Yes, but we should see some signs of reversal in a few minutes. Then she should have a couple of hours after that. Otherwise, she'll need another dose."

"Can we just keep on giving her the vaccine again and again?" asked Owen.

He shook his head. "Nope, sadly that

won't work after the first couple."

"So, what was your other idea?" asked Charlie.

"Well, two things here," he said. "One is as you suggested, let her turn and not worry about it. The other two options are related." He paused.

"So, what are they?" asked Owen, pulling his t-shirt up over his nostrils so he didn't have to smell the stench.

Charlie seemed unaffected. She was a zlayer after all.

"Well, if we let her turn, then kill off the other zleader, that will mean she's in our court," he said.

"What? How would that even work? Once a zombie, always a zombie."

"Not necessarily," said Allan. "The only reason the other zleaders have been against us is because they've always turned in private. Kind of due to embarrassment."

"So, we keep her locked up and hang out with her?" asked Owen.

"Exactly. Though this is just a theory," he said.

"So, you want to turn our friend into a zleader?" Charlie pondered the thought. "It could just work. Just imagine, we'd have all the remaining zombies pouring in. We could kill them off, then be done with this forever."

"Right," Allan said. "But there is one more thing."

The students stared at him.

"It's possible that Zan will have some immunity to zombie bites," said Principal Allan.

"Wait a minute, how would you know that?" asked Charlie.

"Just some history," said Allan. "There have been cases, or so it's been said, that some zlayers are immune."

"That's great," said Charlie. "All this time I've been worried about being bitten and I didn't have to be!"

"Well, don't get too confident. It's just a theory," said Allan. "And there may be spells associated with that immunity."

"Wait a minute," said Owen. "How do you know so much about zombie slaying anyway?"

"Well, isn't it evident?" said Zan, perking up. Her eyes were glowing green, but her skin had returned to its normal healthy pink coloring. "He's a mentor."

"What?" said Charlie. "Who are you

mentoring?"

There was silence for a few seconds. "Sadly, my zlayer student got killed about two years ago. I haven't been mentoring anyone for a while now," explained Allan.

The car slowed down, and then stopped.

"Hey, why are we stopping?" asked Owen.

"Not certain," said Charlie. "There appears to be a closure ahead."

"Hey, where are you?" Charlie texted to Stewart.

"Can't get out of the city," he texted back.

"Great. Stewart is stuck inside the city."

There appeared to be several long winding rows of vehicles trying to get into the city. On the other side, many vehicles were heading out, but at least it wasn't blocked. As they waited, they saw a police officer, wearing a bright fluorescent orange and yellow vest, walking down between the lanes of traffic. At regular intervals, he'd stop and chat with some of the vehicles' drivers. Some of them he directed to turn around. The median was flat grass, so it was easy enough to do a U-turn and get onto the other side of the freeway.

Finally, the cop reached their vehicle.

Charlie rolled down the window. "What's up?" she asked. "We're coming back from a school camping trip and need to get home to our parents."

"Hi there, folks. Unfortunately, we have a confirmed zombie outbreak in the city. I'm here to inform you that it's not safe. You're far safer out here. Do you have any relatives you can visit until it's over?"

Overhead, several helicopters flew, each touring the perimeter. Occasionally, one would lower to the ground and shots would be fired.

"Wait a minute, how did this happen when Tonia was with us?" asked Owen quietly.

"She must have bitten some folks back in the city before we left on our trip," whispered Allan. "So, officer, are we allowed into the city or not?"

The officer frowned. "You are, but it's at your own peril."

"Thank you, officer," said Allan.

Charlie rolled the window back up. By now, they were the next car in the queue. Ahead of them was clear sailing. Some vehicles had decided to go on ahead, while others drove onto the grass and made U-turns out.

"OK, what's the plan then?" asked Charlie.

"Well, we go in and fight," said Principal Allan. "Is everyone in?"

"Wait. We're going back into Portland. What about Tonia?" asked Charlie.

Allan smiled. "Don't worry. Like I said before, I'm a hundred percent confident that she's heading back to the big city too."

Charlie pulled out her phone again. She texted to Stewart. "We're back in the city now. We'll meet you at the school and plan our attack."

"Excellent," he texted back. "I've just accessed a big store of weapons under the school."

"Really?" she texted. "Principal Allan is going to be pissed." She smiled.

ZZZ

It was a cumbersome drive back to Portland High School. They had to stop the car and take turns driving a few times so Charlie or Allan could jump out and kill a zombie or two.

"I don't understand why the infection is so fast," said Charlie. "I haven't seen anything like this before. Usually, it's gradual, over several months."

"I have a feeling that something has sped it up. Not sure what, though," said Allan. "Does Stewart have the spell book?"

"Yes, he does, but he's very protective of it and usually keeps it hidden."

"I understand," he said. "I actually had a copy, but someone destroyed it. I've had to rely on my memory ever since then."

"That's sucks," commented Charlie. "We can make a copy of it for you," she suggested.

"That would be fantastic," he said.

The car made it to the school. Allan parked it in the back, in the teachers' parking area.

"OK, everyone be careful," he said, as they exited the car.

They headed to the back entrance of the school. Principal Allan carefully opened the door. Out jumped three zombies.

Everyone quickly backed away, but soon Charlie, Zan, and Allan had their daggers out. The zombies were quickly dispatched.

"Hey, you can still fight," commented Charlie to Zan.

"Yeah. I actually feel more confident. Like I can understand them or something," she explained.

"OK, keep an eye out," said Allan. "Let's go find Stewart, as we need to see that book and find out what the heck is going on."

"Over here," called Stewart. "That should have been the last of them. I've been fighting zombies all day long."

The group headed over to where he was standing. He led them down the stairs to the bottom. At the very bottom, he pulled a set of keys from his pants pocket. He found an old brass key and opened up the dark metal door there.

"I didn't even know that was down here," said Owen.

They followed Stewart inside. He flicked on the light switch. Once they were all in, he closed and locked the door.

They walked down a long hallway that spanned the length of the school. Unlike the floors above, the walls and ceiling hadn't been painted in years, and the floors were filthy and covered with leaves.

"Good job finding the weapons," said

Allan to Stewart.

"I brought the book from my safety deposit box," said Stewart. "We'll make you a copy as soon as we can."

Finally, they reached the end of the hallway. Stewart unlocked the room at the end. They all headed inside. He flicked the switch on.

The room lit up. On every wall were cases and cases of zombie hunting weapons.

"Wow! This is impressive," said Charlie. "I'd like to try some of these out."

"You can," said Stewart. "But first, I have a gift for you." He removed a box from the table and handed it to her.

"Oh my god," she said, opening it up. "It's the dagger!"

"That's right. This is a special dagger that can kill the zleader. But you must remember to use it only once, and use it only on her, no one else," Stewart explained. "It's important to keep the dagger in its sheath until you need it. You do not want Tonia to see it before you have a chance to use it. She might be able to steal it or destroy it first. It's also been enchanted so you must only use it for its one true purpose."

Charlie carefully removed the package

from the wooden box. Stewart took it from her, tossing the box on an old shelf, as it was no longer required.

Charlie peered at the knife's hilt. It was inside a sheath of brown leather. To look at it, you would not know there was anything special about it. The hilt was made of titanium, making it a dull silver color. It had a texturized surface, likely to make holding the dagger much easier in the hand.

Charlie slid the dagger out of its sheath. The blade was sharp, polished to a high shine. "Wow," she said. "Very nice."

"OK, stop playing with it," said Stewart.

She quickly re-sheathed it and carefully attached it to her belt so it couldn't accidentally slip out. There was something extremely familiar about this dagger.

"OK, what do we know about this zombie uprising?" asked Principal Allan. "There are an unusual number of zombies on the loose."

"Right," said Stewart, going to the table where a large book sat. The book looked like it was from centuries ago. The cover was made from real leather and had small cracks and peels in it. It was a deep dark red but faded in many spots. Strange gold letters were printed on its surface. The words were in Latin so Charlie didn't know what they said.

Stewart flipped the book to the page that had a large red bookmark in it. Covering the page were multiple colorful illustrations of zombies in various states of decay.

"All right," Stewart said. "We're on the pertinent page."

Everyone stood looking expectantly at him.

"This book already mentions everything we know about the zleader. Usually they are female, and they are born when the last zleader bites them and dies. Usually that is the intention, as biting and then eating someone will disqualify them from being a leader. After a new leader is born, they move into a new city. The zleader eventually regenerates their wounds or anything that would make them resemble a zombie so that they can fit in as a human," explained Stewart.

"OK, so where is the part about raising all these zombies?" asked Charlie.

"Yes, here it is. More zombies are made when the zleader bites a human. A human who turns into a zombie can also bite other humans and turn them into zombies. Apparently, the zleader has some sort of influence over her zombies. My best guess is that she's encouraging zombies to create more zombies at a faster pace, as she is aware that the uprising failed in Texas," he explained.

CHAPTER 10

"OK, that sort of explains stuff," said Charlie. "Now, what do we do about Zan?"

Zan had been fairly cheerful up to that point, but now her skin was turning gray. Her lips were pulling back from her mouth, and her eyes were still glowing green.

"Oh, it's simple," said Stewart. "Zlayers are partially immune to turning. With the right spell, we can reverse the process."

Owen nodded enthusiastically. "Let's do it!" he said.

"OK, but we need the death of a human first," said Stewart, reading from the book.

"Great," said Charlie. "Why are these spells so difficult to do?"

"It's magic, Charlie," explained Stewart. "If anyone could do them, imagine how chaotic the world would be."

"Umm," said Charlie.

Everyone laughed.

Principal Allan paced the room, thinking. "OK, what if it's someone who is near death?" he asked.

"That might work, but it has to be someone who is between dying and turning," said Stewart. "They can't already be dead and they can't already be a zombie."

"On it," said Principal Allan, grabbing one of the weapons on the way out.

"OK, let's prepare the rest of the spell," said Stewart.

"I'll go with him," said Owen. "Two people looking are better than one."

Charlie led Zan over to a chair and carefully tied her to it.

"Here, measure these ingredients out carefully," said Stewart. She did as she was told.

A few minutes later, a small table had several small vials on it. In the center was a small black cauldron, with a small Bunsen burner beneath it.

Charlie glanced at Zan. "So, if we do this spell, it will reverse her zombiosis?" she asked.

"Yes," Stewart said.

She nodded enthusiastically. "Good. Too

bad the spell won't reverse all zombies," she commented.

"No, we're not miracle workers," said Stewart. "We still have to kill the zleader in order to kill all of her minions. However, the spell does cover the immediate vicinity, so we can at least reverse the zombie subject and anyone they have recently bitten."

Just then, the power went out.

She could hear Stewart rummaging around the shelves. Soon, a candle was lit.

"I was wondering when that was going to happen," he said. "I do believe we are in stage four of our zombie infestation."

"That's crazy," she said. "It's never progressed this far."

He nodded. "I wonder how the others are doing upstairs."

zzz

Upstairs, Principal Allan and Owen carefully wandered the school, seeking survivors. They found one kid who didn't look too far-gone. He was in one of the younger grades. His eyes weren't turning green yet. Principal

Allan carefully picked him up and slung him over his shoulder. "Quick, let's get back to the basement," he instructed. He and Owen headed to the stairwell.

zzz

All went well as they carefully headed down the stairs, until they heard strange noises coming after them. They tried to move faster, but the footsteps sped up.

They were on the last set of stairs when they saw the monstrosity behind them. It was a zombie, in a fairly advance stage of decomposition. The pair moved faster, but the zombie moved faster too.

"Quick!" said Principal Allan. "We have to make it back to Stewart."

Owen let him go ahead. It was imperative for Allan to get the student to Stewart, as he held the key to saving Zan.

Owen pulled his dagger from inside his jacket pocket and got ready. The final step took the zombie close to him. He plunged the dagger into its head. It had little effect.

"Darn it," said Owen. "Not deep

enough." He raised the dagger again and plunged it into its eye socket. Still, it kept moving.

"Ahhh!" cried Owen. "It bit me!"

"Damn!" said Principal Allan, but he didn't help. Instead, he pulled the door open and raced down the hallway, leaving Owen to fend for himself.

Owen raised the dagger one more time and this time managed to plunge it hard into the zombie's skull, half in anger, and half in fear. It worked. The zombie dropped to the ground, dead.

Owen followed Principal Allan back to the basement storage room.

"Just in time!" cried out Stewart. "Quick, get him over here!" He had a syringe in his hand. He quickly stuck it into the zombie's neck. Then he raced over to the table and carefully squeezed it into one of the vials there.

"Oh my god!" cried Charlie. "Owen's been bitten!" She carefully led him to a chair, and then grabbed a first-aid kit to treat his wound.

"No time for that," said Stewart. "This will destabilize fast. OK, I'm going to add them to the main pot, one at a time."

"There. That's it," he said. Then he raised his voice to do an incantation. "Nolite ortum a immortui," he said.

At first, it seemed as though nothing happened. Then a green swirling mist rose up from the pot. It lifted into the air and headed toward the ceiling. Finally, it was gone.

"So, that's it?" asked Owen. "Did anything happen?"

The group looked around the room.

Zan sat in her chair, looking human. Her eyes had reverted back to their normal brown color. The student was lying in another chair, dazed, but he had zero zombie traits.

"I do think it's worked!" said Stewart.

"Yes, definitely," said Principal Allan. "Now, if you'll excuse me, I have to get home to check on my wife and kids. I'd say it was fun, but I hope you'll be able to handle things from now on."

"Of course," said Stewart.

"Wait!" called Zan. "Does this mean you'll be my mentor?" she asked.

"No, you're on your own," explained Principal Allan. "I don't do that any more."

"Great," she said. "Say, can someone get

these stupid ropes off me?"

Owen rushed over to her and removed the ropes.

"Owen, can you get that student back upstairs? The fewer questions asked, the better," Stewart said.

"Yeah, of course." Owen went over and helped the groggy student up. "Take it easy," he said. "You just drank too much." Soon they were gone from the storage room.

Getting back to business, Charlie spoke up. "We need to figure out where Tonia could be hiding out."

"Yes," he said. "We can't forget she's still out there. What I can do is go through her files in the office upstairs. We can start with where she lives, for one thing."

Charlie helped Stewart to clean up. He placed the spell book back in his briefcase to return to the safety deposit box. He made a note to remind himself that he still had to copy the contents of the book for Principal Allan, even if he was a reluctant mentor.

"Hey, are you feeling better?" Charlie asked Zan.

She nodded. "I just want to sleep for a hundred years. Say, I didn't eat anyone, did

I?" she asked.

"Yep, but he was one of the bad guys, so that's all right."

"Ha-ha. Very funny," she said, laughing. She managed to stand up, feeling a bit unsteady. "Any chance we can sleep now? I think I've been going for 48 hours."

"Yeah, you and everyone else. I think the city is on its own for a few hours while we sleep," Charlie said.

"I'll just finish up here, then we can have Owen drop Zan off at home, while I get you home."

"OK," Charlie said. "I'm glad I had the excuse that I was away at camp. Otherwise, I'd never be able to explain this to Gran."

Footsteps were heard in the corridor. The three tensed, but then relaxed when it was only Owen coming back in.

"What's it like out there?" asked Charlie.

"Messy," he said. "Blood everywhere. But a lot of the students are fine. I've told everyone to go home."

Stewart nodded. "That's good. Let's get out of here before the police arrive. I don't know how anyone is going to explain it all."

Zan followed Owen to his car and hopped in. Soon, they were on their way home.

Charlie hopped in Stewart's car. "Thanks for driving me home. I feel so tired and shaky that I don't think I can drive."

"No problem. It's been a long weekend. Just crazy. I'm so glad we stopped the uprising, at least temporarily. Now that it's done, it seems far more manageable to deal with a zombie or two."

"Yep," she said. "Tomorrow I'll just go around and hunt the few remaining ones left. I can do that, yeah."

Stewart drove in silence for the rest of the trip. Charlie kept on nodding off.

"OK, here we are," he said, pulling into her driveway.

"Great, I'm looking forward to seeing Gran… shit!" she said, kicking open the door of the car. She raced out and ran to the front of the house. Stewart raced after her.

"Now, be careful," he said, as she threw open the front door and raced into the house.

"Gran! Gran!" she yelled.

"In here, dear," said Gran.

Gran was in the living room setting up an elaborate display on the table, involving lit candles, incense, and herbs.

"Did you see?" Charlie started to ask.

"I saw it, dear. Someone painted 'I know where you live' on the outside of the house in blood."

"I'll go and wash it off," said Stewart. He left the house and headed to the garden hose outside.

"You're all right then?"

"Of course, dear. You don't get to be 65 years old by being stupid."

The setup on the table looked like it was for spells.

"How do you know all this?" she asked.

"You pick stuff up as you get older," she explained. "Some knowledge and power is hidden, even from the greatest zlayers."

"You mean spell stuff? Like Stewart?" exclaimed Charlie.

"In a manner of speaking, dear," she said. "Fighting evil runs in our bloodline as far back as we can trace it. Your mother fought before you, just as I did before her."

"Really? I had no idea." Charlie sank onto the couch.

"Yep, retired now, obviously."

Stewart came back inside. "I've removed the marks from the house. I see that the inside is well protected. You have some protection now, but I suggest that you both be careful. Perhaps you should stay somewhere else tonight," Stewart suggested.

"Nah, we'll be fine. If you've magically erased the blood, then the zleader won't easily find her way back here. She's smart, but each day she loses just a little bit more of her reasoning power," explained Gran.

"Say, is there a lifespan for a zleader?" asked Charlie. "I've always wondered."

Stewart nodded. "Usually about a year."

She did the math. "Darn it. It's not that far along then."

"Well, the last thing we need to worry about is a new zleader. At least we have some info about this one."

Charlie started nodding off on the couch.

"OK, let her rest," said Gran.

Stewart agreed and left the house. He made sure she closed and locked all of the doors and windows before driving away. Inside, Gran put a cozy blanket over Charlie, as she had collapsed in her chair, fast asleep.

During the night, she carefully tended the candles, keeping watch.

CHAPTER 11

"It's good to get back into the routine again," said Charlie. The school was minus several students and teachers though. There were services being held on the weekend. Charlie enjoyed hanging out with Zan and Owen. She knew that eventually Tonia, the zleader, would be up to no good and her presence would be made known again.

So far there hadn't been much in the news. They said it had been a typhoid fever outbreak, caused by a family coming back from Mexico. They'd infected many other people in Portland and the surrounding cities. But now, everyone was in quarantine and the infected water system had been thoroughly drained and cleaned. Things should be reverting back to normal.

Charlie shook her head, thinking that they should just be honest with what was happening in the world today. It was a zombie plague, not typhoid fever. In fact, typhoid was much deadlier and quicker.

"So, any plans for the weekend?" asked Owen.

"Not sure," she answered. "I might just chill out or something. Last week was a bit too intense."

"I know what you mean. My parents flipped out. They want to permanently ground me or something."

"Right," she said, laughing. "Because being in school is a hundred percent safe."

"Yeah, I told them how some students died at the campsite and the school. They were quiet after that. Any sighting of you-know-who?"

She shook her head. "Nope. She's been lying low. They do get tired like we do."

He smiled. "Well, might as well rest and catch up on schoolwork while we can. Never know when the next strike will be."

"Yep."

"OK, so I'm thinking, Saturday night we should do something normal, like take in a movie."

She smiled. "That's a plan."

"I already asked Zan," he said.

"Good. Oh and you and Zan are welcome to go alone. I'm sure you don't want me to tag along," she said, smirking.

His eyes grew wide. "Oh no, just as friends! She's great and all, but sometimes I can't stand her self-righteousness."

She laughed. "Just kidding. Zlayers can't have normal relationships anyway."

He frowned. "They can't?"

"Nope. Because someone will eventually get killed."

"I see."

"Yep, when I was working Dallas, I had a boyfriend. And he got killed. It was all my fault," she said, opening up. They were seated at the back of bio class. No other students had come in yet.

"I'm sorry to hear that. But how was it your fault? It's not your fault there are zombies and zleaders. You didn't directly kill him."

"Well, I needed bait and instead of sending someone in with experience, I sent him in. I was mad at him for forgetting my birthday. I did it out of spite. After he was gone, I really blamed myself."

He shook his head. "You couldn't have known that. You were only mad. Sounds to me like it was his fault. Isn't there that old saying, 'you reap what you sow'?"

She sighed. "Well, yes, I know. His actions led to it. But then, so did mine. Anyway, thanks for listening," she said, as the first students came into the classroom.

"If you want to talk about it some more, then let me know." He sat back and flipped open his notebook.

zzz

"This is a great idea," said Zan. "I haven't been out in ages. Though I hope this isn't a zombie flick."

"Nah," said Owen. "Oh, and I watched some this week. They are hilarious. Not quite like real life," he explained.

Charlie smirked knowingly. "Maybe that can be my adult career. Zombie expert," she said.

"Hey, good one!" said Zan. "You can charge $1,200 per hour, like lawyers do."

Charlie smiled.

They enjoyed watching their non-zombie movie, but it was mostly an action flick with little plot line to it. However, it was just what the teens needed to wind down after a tough week. Charlie was surprised to see Owen adapting so well. She wondered if he was going to turn into a zlayer. After all, they all had to start somewhere.

In the beginning, she had killed one or two zombies. Then, Stewart had initiated contact, saying that she was a zlayer. Once you were chosen, you had no options. It was your calling and you had to do it. The time to back down was earlier, when you could call the cops instead of killing the zombies.

The credits had just started rolling when the power went out.

"Hey!" said Zan.

"What the?" asked Owen.

Charlie was already up and out of her chair. She pulled her dagger from the back of her pants pocket. She always had it on her, no matter what. The other dagger was tucked inside a belt that pressed up against her skin. She kept that one concealed.

Most of the theater's attendees quickly left the room. Some used their cellphones as flashlights to navigate their way out.

"Excuse me, what's going on?" asked a young woman. She was with her boyfriend, who was holding up his smartphone.

Owen chuckled.

"The power has gone out," said Charlie. "I think we just need to leave so they can fix the issue."

They headed into the lobby.

"My name is Sara, and this is Ce," she told them.

Charlie was distracted. She wasn't here to make friends. She wanted to make sure that everyone would be safe. "Err, hi, Ce. That's an unusual name."

"It's short for Cedar," said the guy.

"Cool," said Owen. "I'm Owen, and that's Charlie and Zan." They all shook hands.

zzz

The group headed into the lobby. Most of the people had left by now. After a minute or two, the lights came back on again. Everyone breathed a sigh of relief.

"Say, it was fun meeting you," said Charlie. "Let's get together for a movie in the future," she said. It would be nice to hang out with normal people for a change.

The couple waved at them and left.

"See ya!" said Zan, heading to her car.

"Oh man, I think I have PTSD or something. I thought we were doomed," said Owen.

"I know," said Charlie. "I don't trust when anything goes wrong anymore. I'm always jumpy. That's why I want to retire from this."

"Don't blame you," said Owen. "Me too."

"Oh, it's easy for you. Just say no," she said.

"But my friends are at risk," he said.

She smiled, grateful to have a friend who had her back.

"I still feel a bit bad for bailing out on you before though." They headed to her car. She'd driven it home from school the day after all the excitement happened.

"Please, say no more. I'd have done the same." She thought for a bit. "I think there's something I need to ask Gran."

"OK. I'll see you at school on Monday." She stopped the car in front of his house. They both said their goodbyes.

Charlie drove home and parked her car in

the driveway, and then carefully exited her vehicle. She peered around, but there were no zombies. Gran's house was as clean and pristine as Stewart had left it the other night. But she knew Tonia wouldn't just come charging out at them. The zombie was smart.

"Umm, wait," she said to herself. "How had she known to come here? Does she know I'm a zlayer? And if so, how did she figure it out?" She pondered the issue. She sat on the front steps of her house. Tonia had seen her at the camp. But that wasn't any indication that she was a zlayer. She hadn't had the special dagger. And she wasn't the only Oregonian who carried around knives and daggers, let alone guns.

"Eff it," she said to herself. "Someone told her who I am."

"Hi, dear," said Gran, coming out onto the porch. "Who told her?" she asked.

"Gran, it's not a coincidence that we've been targeted. I believe someone told Tonia I'm a zlayer. They get off on these things."

"I know, dear. I wanted to tell you the other night, but you were exhausted. And even if someone tipped her off, she would have figured it out eventually." Gran gave her a hug, which she willingly took.

"So, who could it have been? Is it possible that Zan is still tied to the zombies, despite the reverse spell?"

"I don't think so," said Gran.

"Then there is Owen, Stewart, Principal Allan, and Ben. I just can't see it," she said.

"I'm sure you'll figure it out eventually," Gran said.

"Well, it worries me. It's like the zombies are up to something," she said.

Gran nodded knowingly. "The zombies are always up to something. It's like they want to conquer the world."

"Say, Gran. I have a question for you."

"Yes, dear?"

"How old were you when you retired? I mean, from zombie slaying?"

"Back then, there were more than just zombies, but if you want to know... Let's see," she said. "I tried a few times but then went back to it. I think I was 32 years old when I stopped."

"Wait. More than just zombies?" Charlie questioned.

"Stories for another time, dear," Gran replied.

"That's fine, I guess. And you were 32?!"

Charlie exclaimed. "Darn it, that's a long time."

"It should have been sooner, but there weren't enough people like us back then. And there have been zombies as far back as the 18th century, at least that I'm aware of. It's believed that they are a human creation."

Charlie looked at her. "I don't doubt it. Still, I was hoping I could retire a lot sooner and lead a normal life."

"I know. Perhaps you can clear up this infestation, kill the zleader, and get back to your schoolwork."

Charlie smiled.

zzz

Charlie's phone got a text. She picked it up and looked at it.

"Hey, movie at 2 pm on Saturday?" texted Sara.

"Yeah," Charlie texted back. "How did you get my #?"

"From Owen," texted Sara. "He's in the same calculus class as Ce."

"Perfect," she texted back, then closed

her phone.

She headed off to her meeting with Stewart. At his house, they chatted about Tonia.

"OK, so Tonia knows where you live. Let's see if we can figure out as much information about her as she knows about you," said Stewart.

"Well, she's at our school. I don't know much more than that," she replied.

Stewart picked up a legal folder and flipped through the papers inside.

"She's a cheerleader, apparently, or at least was, until she quit last week. She's been at the high school since 10th grade. She's originally from Seattle. Generally, she does well in class, mostly As and Bs, but her marks have taken a dive this past week. She also has attendance issues."

"Well, that's the norm for a zleader," said Charlie. "Did she even show up for class the past couple of days?"

He shook his head.

"Darn. I guess it won't be easy finding her."

"I suggest we head to her house to see if she's there," said Stewart.

She nodded. "Great." She stood up,

patting herself down to make sure she had both of her daggers on her. "I'd like to deliver the final blow so we can get back to normal again."

Stewart smiled. "I'll leave you to it. I have to grade some papers."

Charlie stomped to the door. "That's just great," she said, as she took the slip of paper that Stewart handed to her. "And it's friggin' in Vancouver. It's going to be an all-night investigation." She opened the door.

"Good luck," Stewart called after her. "Don't forget…"

"To check in," she completed his sentence for him. She left.

zzz

"Stupid Vancouver," said Charlie, driving to the address on the small slip of paper. "Might as well be in Vancouver, Canada." It was during rush hour traffic so movement was slow. She finally was able to cross the bridge, leave Oregon, and enter the Vancouver in Washington State.

"Geez, why do people live over here and

commute to school?" She knew that many of the students and teachers had at least a 45-minute commute each day, longer if they got stuck in traffic.

She finally found the address and drove by the driveway. The house wasn't as well kept as Gran's house was and all of the decorative foliage was overgrown. She decided to park the car a block away so she could discreetly go in if she had to.

CHAPTER 12

"I'm going in," she texted Stewart.

"Good," he said. "Let me know if you need anything." She put her phone away, got out of her car, and pretended she was only walking down the street.

The first time she simply walked past. It appeared to be like any other house on the block. She headed around the block to check to see if there was a back alley, but there wasn't. It was a crowded urban layout where residents parked their cars on the street. She returned from the direction she had arrived.

Charlie walked up the steps to knock on the door. There was no response. She tried three times, peering in through the glass window at the top of the door, and then leaning over the side to peer in through the larger window. She decided to try the doorbell. No response. She walked down the steps and checked out the back. In the back, there was a small open carport with no vehicle in it.

She headed to the back door and tried the knob. It opened. Glancing around quickly, she went inside. She closed the door behind her so she wouldn't draw attention to the house.

Inside, she quickly found the light switch. She flicked it on. "What the?" she said.

In front of her were three people tied up and on the ground. She raced up to one of them and pulled off the duct tape covering her mouth.

"Oh, thank god! We've had no food or water for three days!"

Charlie quickly undid the ropes binding her hands, and then untied the father and son who were also tied up. She helped rid them of duct tape and ropes.

She raced into the bathroom just off to the side and found a glass. She turned on the tap and let it fill the glass. She quickly raced back out and handed the water to the child first. They each took sips.

"What happened?" asked Charlie.

"Oh my god. Our teenage daughter

tricked us. She got us down here and then tied us up."

"Was it Tonia?" asked Charlie.

"Yes," said the father.

"She's never acted up before," said the mom.

"Well, we have to notify the police," said Charlie. "She's gone too far." She dialed 911 and placed the call. Now that there was good reason to contact the police, they could be on the lookout for a teenage girl bearing her description. More eyes meant that she would be found sooner.

When the MISSING warning went out, it also bore the disclaimer "armed and dangerous. Notify the police and do not approach."

Fortunately, none of the family had been bitten. Charlie didn't even mention to the paramedics that was a possibility.

"OK, if we're done here, I'm heading home," said Charlie.

"Yes, thank you for helping," said Sergeant Bourne.

Charlie walked back to her car. Another dead end.

"Well, I managed to rescue the family, but Tonia was not in sight."

"OK, well, try her workplace next," he suggested.

"Do you know where that was?" she asked.

"I can find out," he said. He called back two minutes later.

"OK, so she worked at a place called The Bean Trip on Main Street."

"Argh!" she said. "Everything is connected together."

"Oh, you already have a lead?" he asked.

"Yep, on it," she said as she hung up. "OK, what was the name of that guy who worked the shop? Umm, Steve, the barista, that's it. Shoot, but I don't know his last name. Hmmm."

She hated driving in downtown Portland, so she parked her car blocks away where she didn't have to pay the Parking Kitty. It's not like she got reimbursed for expenses after all. Though she didn't really need to be reimbursed. She was set in her old ways, even if she didn't have to worry as much about money now that she lived with Gran.

She walked on foot. She passed the big block of Main Street Books, and then headed across the street to where The Bean Trip had been. Part of the building still remained, charred and burned out.

She walked up, waving her hand in front of her face. There was a strong smell of burnt wood in the air along with a big condemned notice attached to what remained of the door. Beside it, another notice thanked all their customers, but the owner had decided to retire and wished everyone the best. The owner was just listed as Eli.

A few doors down was a small clothing store. Charlie headed that way.

She entered the store and heard the bell ring above her.

"Hi," she said to the store clerk. "Do you know Eli or Steve who worked at the coffee shop next door?"

"Hi," said the man behind the cash register. "That would be Eli Moon. He left for Seattle with the insurance money saying he wouldn't be back. Why?" he asked. He was tidying the countertop.

"I found a wallet belonging to Steve," said

Charlie, lying. "But his ID has his old address on it. I need to find out where he lives, or if he works somewhere else."

"Oh, that's nice," the clerk said. "I heard he works at the supermarket down the street now."

"That's great. Thank you," she said, peering behind him. There was a backpack on the back counter. It was open with its contents spilling onto the surface.

She frowned. "Say, that's not zrug, is it?" she asked.

The clerk frowned, then smiled. "It is, but it's all mine. It's the last of it since that shop shut down. I don't know where else to get it. Any ideas?" he asked, flinging his scarf back.

"No. You should find some weed instead. That stuff'll turn you into a zombie," she suggested.

She left the shop, now on the hunt for the supermarket down the street.

zzz

"Hello, remember me?" said Charlie.

Steve nearly jumped out of his skin when

he saw her. "Say, umm, hi," he said, pushing his bangs back.

"Hi," she said, smiling at him.

"What's up?" he asked. He leaned in close to her. "I don't make or sell drugs any more."

"It's not that," she said. "I was wondering if you know Tonia?"

"Tonia?"

"Yep. High school girl, 11th grade. Has blonde hair, is short and petite. Has an attitude. Is a zombie."

"I thought you killed them all," he whispered back at her, nervously peering around the meat counter.

"Nope. I'm looking specifically for her."

He shook his head. "I haven't seen her, only worked with her. We don't socialize at all."

"Darn it," she said. "My leads are going nowhere." She handed him a card. "If you hear anything from her or about her, I'd appreciate it if you gave me a call."

He nodded.

She left and headed back to her car. This left only one lead open to her. She was going to have to go and visit Stan and John again. If they were still selling the zrug, then they must know a bit more about their sources and, possibly, Tonia's whereabouts.

She drove around the corner, as their dumpy apartment building wasn't that far from the supermarket and coffee shop. She parked a block away and gave a homeless man some change.

Then, she headed for the alley with the apartment. She quickly picked the main entrance lock and walked in.

She quietly moved to the drug dealers' door, and then tried the doorknob. It was locked. She pulled the brooch off of her jacket again and flipped the long pin out. She used it to pick the door lock. It was fairly simple. These doors hadn't been updated, and only had a simple lock in the doorknob rather than a deadbolt lock, which was nearly impossible to pick unless you had taken a long and complex lock-picking course.

The lock clicked open. She listened but couldn't hear voices on the other side of the door.

She flung the door wide. Inside was John, on the telephone.

"Hey," he said to her, confused. "I'll get to you when I'm done this call."

"Oh, no rush," she replied. "Whenever you have time." She wandered around the small room. It had old furniture but was surprisingly clean for a drug dealer's den.

She knew she was onto something when she saw a picture of Tonia in one of the picture frames above the fireplace. "Say, is this girl one of your girlfriends?" she asked, turning back to face John.

But before she could fully turn to face him, she felt a blow to her head. She struggled to remain conscious. She moved her arms forward to protect her face from hitting the floor. The pain was intense. She struggled, kicking out. Her leg connected with something, but soon she lost consciousness.

zzz

When she awoke, Steve was hanging over her. "Hey, man. Sorry to do this to you, but you got too nosy."

"Geez, Steve. I told you that I'm not interested in the drugs," she said, struggling against the ropes that bound her arms.

"I know. You're interested in the zombies."

"Where are John and Stan?" she asked, looking around.

"They scrammed. They don't get involved in the dirty stuff," he explained.

"So, where is Eli?" asked Charlie, working against her bonds.

"He's scrammed. He doesn't need us anymore. Anyway, he wasn't good at moving product."

"So what's the point of this?" she asked. "Keeping me here?"

"Why did you come here?" he asked.

"To find Tonia, obviously." She shook her head in the direction of the photo.

"Oh her, right. You don't want to mess with her. Now me, on the other hand, she has promised me immortality." Steve went to sit on the other side of the room.

"Really?" she replied. "Did she tell you that you'd be dead?"

"Of course," he said. "Then we will rise together!"

"That's not all that was rising, apparently," she joked. "Listen up. She'll turn you into nothing more than a zombie who feeds on the souls of the living.

Eventually, you'll drop down to the ground in a mass of dead flesh and bones and you'll be gone."

"Nah, that's not what she said." He took out his knife and started playing with it.

"It's true. I'm a zlayer. I should know."

He smiled. "She was right about you. She can pick out a zlayer from a mile away. You and that Zan girl."

"Oh, Zan has nothing to do with any of this," said Charlie, managing to loosen the ropes wrapped around her wrists. You had to loosen them against the grain. Otherwise, they'd just tighten up even more.

"Liar," he said. "Anyway, doesn't matter. She's on her way to kill Zan."

"What?!" she cried. "No!"

"Yep."

"Wait, how does Tonia know where I live, or where Zan lives for that matter?"

"Oh, someone's making money on the side," he said.

"Money? Who do I know who needs money? Hmmm."

"Well, I'm sure you'll be able to guess," he said. "We'll just wait here until Tonia gets back, and then she can eat you herself."

"I heard that zlayers are bad for the

stomach," she said, smirking.

He laughed.

"Seriously, either you're a zombie, a zombie slayer, or the zombie leader. There is nothing else. There is no zombie boyfriend in this world."

"Oh, she told me there is a way."

Charlie looked at him, expecting more. By now, she could have thrown off the poorly tied knots, but she was interested in the conversation.

"A spell," he said.

"Darn it. Someone must have given her the spell," she said.

"Yep," said Steve.

"Dammit, Steve!" Charlie yelled at him. "She's playing two guys!"

Just then, there were some strange sounds coming from outside the door.

"What's going on out there? Did you bring your friends?" he asked. He got up from his chair and headed to the door.

CHAPTER 13

While Steve was peering outside to see what was up, Charlie threw off the ropes. Steve had found the dagger in her back pocket but not the other one. As she walked past the table, she picked it up and put it back inside her pocket.

"Hello!" she said loudly to him, pushing him aside.

He tripped and fell to the ground. "Hey!" he said. "Where are you going?"

But she was already gone.

zzz

"Well, that was a big waste of my time," she muttered to herself as she went to get her car. "But at least I know more of what's happening." She hoped that the romance situation would resolve itself between Steve and Tonia. She didn't think he was really a bad guy, as he hadn't hurt her or touched her at all, beyond tying her up. Perhaps he'd see that the zleader was conning him, and he'd leave.

Now, where would Zan be at this time? Probably at home. She wondered who had told Tonia where Zan lived.

Charlie drove as quickly as she could, without running the red lights or being a target of the speed cameras.

She quickly drove into Zan's driveway. Good thing she'd collected everyone's address as a precaution in her address book. She was going to walk up to her front door, but heard noises coming from the back. She picked up the pace and walked quickly around to the back of the house.

Lying on the ground was Tonia, with Owen and Zan restraining her.

"Nice job, guys," said Charlie. "You don't need me at all."

"Quick!" said Owen. "Use your dagger on her."

"Oh right," said Charlie. "I have it right here. This is going to be easy!"

Tonia struggled on the ground. She was strong, but wasn't a match for two teens who were bigger than her.

Charlie pulled open her jacket and grabbed the dagger. Then she walked over to where Tonia was being pinned down on the ground. She took the dagger and jammed it down hard into her skull.

Everyone waited for her to die. Tonia started having seizures. Her entire body started shaking. All three held her down the best they could.

Finally, she had one last seizure, and then was still.

"Is that it?" asked Owen. "That seemed almost too easy."

Then Tonia's eyes opened, and she sat up. "Oh, stupid!" she cried. "Why did you do that?"

"What the?" said Zan. "You're still alive?"

"Yes, I can't be thwarted that easily," said Tonia.

"What? I thought the special titanium dagger was supposed to kill her?" said Charlie.

"Guess not," said Owen.

Tonia stood up and rushed against everyone. She pushed Zan to the ground.

"Shit! I'd bite you, but you're immune."

"What?" said Zan. "Because you bit me before and I recovered?"

Tonia nodded.

"Hey, me too!" said Owen.

Tonia smiled. "OK, so who hasn't been bitten yet and isn't immune? Hmmm?" She looked in the direction of Charlie.

"Oh crap," said Charlie. She backed away. Zan and Owen had been bitten before, and Stewart had performed the spell, so now they were permanently immune. But Charlie had never been bitten, so she had not benefited from the power of the spell.

She looked at the dagger in her hand. It was fine, and hadn't crumpled when she used it. There was blood on the hilt, but it was still good.

The hole in Tonia's head soon healed over, just like the last time she'd been stabbed back at the campsite.

Charlie rushed forward, stabbing her again and again. This only slowed Tonia down. She stabbed her one more time, and then Zan rushed in and tossed a net over her head. The net was glittery, like it was made from some type of metal threads. Tonia went down.

"Hey, cool," said Owen. "What's that?"

"It's made of titanium," said Zan. "It should hold her for now."

"Wow, that's great," said Charlie, impressed.

The teens gazed down at Tonia. She flailed against the ropes of the netting but to no avail.

"Great. Now we just have to figure out how to kill her." Charlie scratched her head.

They secured the netting to a tree in the backyard.

"Hey, how does she know where I live?" asked Zan.

"We have a traitor in our midst," said Charlie. They looked at Owen.

"Hey! It's not me!" he protested. "I'm on your side."

"OK, we have her tied up. Now what?" asked Zan. "It's not like we can just kill her."

Charlie frowned. "I wonder why the titanium didn't work. Stewart was so certain. OK, I'm calling him."

She took her phone out of her jacket and gave him a call.

"Another late night?" he said, answering the telephone.

"Yep," she said. "Say, any reason why the titanium dagger didn't work?" she asked him.

"What?" he said. "The dagger didn't work?"

"No. We have Tonia on the ground tied up, but the dagger has no effect on her."

Stewart sighed. "Did you say the spell at the same time?"

"What?" she cried. "You said nothing about that!" She hung up. "We have to say the spell as we use the dagger. I swear. He did not tell me that. This is completely different than when I killed the zleader in Texas."

"Great," said Zan. "Even I didn't know that. Are they changing the rules on us?"

"Well, things are definitely changing. One thing for certain is that it's a lot harder to kill a zombie nowadays."

"Hey, ladies," called out Owen. "We have a problem here."

They looked over at him. Owen held up a portion of the titanium netting. Tonia was gone. "While you were yakking, she escaped."

"Crap!" said Charlie. "She's outsmarted us again!"

The teens ran around the yard and checked the house, but Tonia was nowhere to be found.

"Just great," said Zan. "Now what do we do?"

"I think we should get some sleep," said Charlie. "It's going to be a long week. Now we have a zleader who knows where two of us live, and we have a traitor in our midst."

zzz

Charlie had a good night's sleep. She knew that as the days progressed that it would become harder and harder to do that. Gran kept up the protections around the house, and even included the yard. This would keep her house invisible to the zleader and the zombies. She texted Zan to do the same and was told that she'd already done it.

On Monday, one of the teachers announced that there would be a field trip that day.

Charlie raised her hand. "Is that necessary? Look what happened on the camping trip."

"Oh, that's over and done with," explained the teacher.

"It's not," said Charlie. "There are still zombies roaming around out there, and the zleader too."

"Well, this is merely a trip to the local art museum. There are security guards and cameras there. What could go wrong?"

Charlie was annoyed. She was fully aware that a lot could go wrong.

zzz

In one of the art museum's rooms, Charlie reached up and broke the glass of the surveillance camera. Once that was done, she stepped forward and took out the zombie in front of her. In the distance, she heard students and the general public as they raced down the stairs, screaming.

She looked up at the painting in front of her and squinted her eyes. She smiled. "It looks so much better now." The painting now had random blood splatters covering its surface. She wondered how long it would be before anyone noticed. She made it a point to check back next week. Wouldn't it be cool if no one noticed and the painting spent an eternity being covered in zombie splatter, until some future archaeologist decided to do testing on it? She hoped by then that zombies wouldn't be a thing.

She followed the last of the students down the stairs. The upper floors had been cleared out. She exited the building and walked over to where the teacher was standing. She could never remember his name.

"Hey, Mr. Smooch, this was a fantastic field trip! I always enjoy a good zombie hunt."

Mr. Smetch was so flustered by the afternoon that he didn't correct her pronunciation of his name. "Please board the bus and we'll get going."

She didn't board the bus with the rest of the students. Instead, she headed to where her car was parked. Owen and Zan followed suit.

"Wow, that was crazy," said Zan.

"What were the teachers thinking?" asked Owen.

"I'm surprised that Principal Allan allowed this," said Charlie.

"Yeah, unless he's the traitor in our midst," Zan said.

"What?" said Charlie.

"Well, it makes sense," said Zan. "He would have had access to where I live, and where you live."

"Darn it," she said, acknowledging that this could be the case.

zzz

The school staff managed to get everyone safely back to the school, alive. The students were instructed not to tell their parents, otherwise, it would affect their grades.

"Wow," said Owen. "What happened to the olden days when there were actually morals?"

Charlie shrugged. "I think it makes school more fun."

Zan smiled. "I'll say. I took down four zombies at the school!"

"Impressive," said Charlie.

"OK, so school has been dismissed for the rest of the day," said Owen. "Now what?"

"We go back and visit Steve," said Charlie. "Now that we know how to kill Tonia properly, we can hunt her down."

They got in her car and headed to the drug dealers' place. Charlie banged on the door. Steve opened up.

"What?" he said. "I was sleeping."

The trio barged in.

"What the?" he said.

"Where's Tonia?" asked Charlie.

"She ain't here," he said.

"See, I told you that she'd dump you after using you up," said Charlie.

"Nah," he said, using his hands to tidy his hair and pull his shirt down. "She was here last night. Then she left, saying she had errands to do."

"So we'll just hang out here until she returns," said Charlie. "Owen, close the door." He did.

The trio settled down to wait.

zzz

Steve went to have a shower. "Whatever," he thought to himself. Tonia seemed to be able to look after herself. As he was showering, he wondered when she'd turn him into a zombie so that he could be a zombie leader too. He would love to be immortal and have glowing green eyes like hers. He sang as he washed.

zzz

Back in the living room, the team made their plans.

"I really think we should skip school until this is done," said Charlie. "We can't keep on driving back and forth."

Zan tried to get comfortable on the sagging couch. "Terrible, isn't it?" she commented.

"I'm with that," said Owen. "Besides, the kids aren't going to keep quiet about what happened at the art gallery today. Once they blab, their parents will keep them at home, especially after that zombie outbreak last week."

"OK, so here's what we'll do," Charlie said. "There will be two of us here at all times. If I'm not here, I'll give the dagger to

Zan, as she knows what to do. That means that one of us must always be here. Owen, you're the backup." He nodded at her.

"We've got to kill Tonia and get this done. This is ridiculous. I don't think I've had a zombie target for so long in my life. Perhaps I'm getting soft."

Steve came out, drying his hair. "Well, here's your chance," he said. He nodded in the direction of the door. The doorknob was turning.

Everyone jumped out of their chairs. The door opened. It was Tonia.

Charlie extracted the enchanted dagger concealed under her jacket. She rushed at Tonia. She raised the dagger and plunged it into her eye socket. Tonia dropped to the ground.

"Yawn," said Steve. "That does nothing."

CHAPTER 14

Zan covered Tonia with the titanium netting, just in case. All four people stared down at her on the floor. Last time around, she had seizures before resurrecting herself.

Charlie smiled and nodded as the first seizure started. She was almost ready to plunge the dagger into her skull and chant the spell, when the seizures stopped.

"What the?" cried Steve. "Hello?"

"Sorry, Steve," mumbled Tonia. "It's done."

"Done? What's done?" he cried. She wasn't rejuvenating. In fact, the skin all over her body was turning gray. Her contact lens slipped out of her one remaining eye. The once glowing green now burned dully. Her flesh started peeling away from her bones.

"I don't understand," cried Steve. "What's happening?"

The two zlayers and Owen looked at each other. What on earth was going on?

"He made me do it," said Tonia, her words garbled.

"Who made you do it?" asked Steve.

"It was him," she muttered. "He threatened to kill everyone in my family if I didn't do it. I may be a zleader, but I still care about people."

"What the hell?" said Charlie.

Tonia's body gave one last convulsion before she died. Zan quickly used her dagger to ensure that she would not reanimate again. "Should we use your dagger again and do the spell?" she asked Charlie.

Charlie shook her head. "No, she is gone now. Crap. This is bad."

Steve was down by the floor shaking Tonia. "Tonia, come back!" he cried.

"That's so sad," said Zan. "Now I don't know if she was playing or really cared for him." The trio stood up and went to sit on the couch while they watched Steve mourn his loss.

"Well, there may have been some remaining humanity in her. But it's impossible to have two zleaders at once. Unless, oh crap!"

"What is it?" asked Owen.

"Unless, someone lied to her and said it could be done. In that case, I feel a bit bad."

Zan scrunched up her face, cleaning her dagger on the couch. She then put it away. "Do you know how many people have died these past ten days?"

"You're right," said Charlie. "Since you put it that way."

"So, who did it?" said Owen. "Was it Stewart?"

Charlie shook her head. "I've known Stewart for years now. He wouldn't betray the human race. No, this is someone else."

"Shit!" said Zan. "It's Principal Allan."

"Yes," said Charlie. "Because remember when early last week I said he was doing suspicious things? He met up with Tonia at The Bean Trip. I hadn't realized it at the time, but that was her."

Zan and Owen nodded.

"Wait," she said. "I saw you and Allan leaving school later, last week."

"Oh, I was talking to him about the school dance," she said. "Nothing sinister about that."

"There's a school dance?" asked Owen. Zan nodded. He smirked.

"And one other thing. I saw Principal Allan come here."

"So he is connected to this mess then?" asked Zan.

"OK, now what?" asked Owen.

"The next step is to find Principal Allan," said Charlie.

"Oh, so Allan was the one who must have given Tonia that spell so that she couldn't be killed by the titanium," mused Zan.

"Yes," said Charlie, grabbing her bag. The trio headed to the door.

"But, why would he do that when he ultimately wanted to kill her?" asked Owen.

"There is only one reason for it," said Charlie. The others looked at her, waiting for an explanation. "He has thought up an even more diabolical plan."

"Sorry for your loss," said Owen to Steve. They left and closed the door behind themselves.

"I don't think Steve will be any more trouble," said Charlie, when Zan pointed to her dagger and thrust her head to the door.

They walked down the alley and to the car.

"Say, I have another question," said Owen. The others looked at him as they got in the car. "Why do zombies progress at different rates?"

"Oh, you mean decay or intelligence?" asked Zan.

He nodded.

"It's just like with people," said Charlie. "Some people are healthy, some aren't. Humans die at different ages and have different diseases affect them. Zombies are no different. Tonia could have bitten one zombie who died in a day, while she could have bitten another one who'd live for a few months."

"Happy now?" asked Zan.

Owen nodded.

Charlie started the car and headed back to the school. She had been hoping that they'd be able to steer clear of the school, but no such luck. "I guess that Principal Allan remembered some of the spells from the spell book."

"You know what?" said Zan. "I'll bet he's a disgraced mentor and not allowed to practice anymore."

Charlie grimaced. "I think you're right. I've never heard of a mentor turning down a potential zlayer. But he still has the cache of weapons for it."

"Well, we're heading back to school, so we'll figure out what's up," said Owen.

"Right. Say, do you guys mind if you walk the last block? I want to think for a bit."

Owen and Zan looked at each other. "Sure," they said in unison.

As Zan closed the car door, Owen spoke up. "Did you want to go to that dance later this month? I mean, as friends," he said.

Zan smiled.

Charlie just sat in the car, leaving it running. She placed her head on her hands, which were resting on the top of the steering wheel. She had really believed that they had been near the end of their quest. Once Tonia was dead, they wouldn't have to do anything else. Now that was not the case.

Her phone rang.

"Hey! It's me, Stewart," he said.

"Bad news," she said, and told him what had happened. She hung up and went back to sitting in her vehicle. Around her, the streets were quiet. This was quite unusual for Portland, but then, the same thing had occurred when the zombie uprising happened in Dallas, Texas.

"OK, let's get going," she said to herself. She drove to the school and hopped out of her car. Her friends were waiting for her in the parking lot.

"OK, this has to stop now," she said. "Here's what we do. Owen, I need you to drive to the hardware store and buy some bags of salt. When you have them, I want you to pour the salt around the perimeter of the school."

Owen looked horrified. "Are you serious? Do you know how many bags that'll take?"

She laughed. "It only has to be a few grains. Do your best."

"What should I do?" Zan asked.

"I want you to get any staff or students out of here. I expect there are still some lingering, uncertain what to do."

"Got it," said Zan. Her friends headed off on their tasks.

Charlie entered the school. She walked down to the bottom of the stairwell and picked the lock. She then walked down the long hallway to the weapons room. Once there, she picked that door lock too. She opened it and walked inside.

The room was untouched. She wasn't certain if Principal Allan had any use for the weapons, but it was possible that his zombies could use them. She found some oils on the shelf, and combustibles too. She scattered them around the floor. She also found a stash of candles and matches.

She grabbed a few of the daggers and placed them into her backpack. You could never have too many daggers. She pulled open a few drawers. Much of the room seemed to be storage for the rest of the school. Inside one of the drawers were sheets of paper with photocopied cartoon characters on them. In others, she found quizzes and tests. Some drawers had endless amounts of pens and pencils. She even found a dead rat on one shelf.

She briefly thought of grabbing it. It may come in handy for a spell or two. She was getting better at the spells, but mostly would let Stewart handle them. After all, she had misunderstood about the spell associated with the titanium dagger. Either that, or Stewart's mind was slipping.

She looked wistfully at the weapons on the walls and shelves. She really wished that she could save them all. But after she gave it more thought, in the wrong hands, they could hurt a lot of people. The weapons had no place in the basement of the school. Whatever being was responsible for the mentors, they would be immensely displeased if they knew that Principal Allan had placed all these weapons beneath the school.

She lit the match and touched it to several candles. She then tossed the match in the air, and tipped over all the candles. She watched as the fire took hold. This not only solved the problem of the weapons, but would also draw Principal Allan out of the school.

When the flames were well on their way, she headed for the door. She turned the knob but it caught. "Dammit!" she said. Someone had locked or jammed the door somehow. She turned and looked behind her. The fire had reached the essential oils that she'd poured on the floor. The flames tripled in seconds.

CHAPTER 15

"Where is she?" asked Owen frantically. Owen and Zan smelled smoke and ran up and down the hallways of the school looking for Charlie.

"She wouldn't be in the basement would she?" asked Zan.

They raced to the stairwell and down the stairs.

"Did you have a chance to spread the salt?" asked Zan.

"Yep, to the best of my ability. Good thing the store was only a minute's drive away."

The door to the hallway at the bottom was open and unlocked.

"Did you see Principal Allan anywhere yet?" Owen asked her.

The students raced down the hallway to the weapons room. As they approached, the smoke was getting much thicker.

"Yep," she said. "He was in his office. He didn't see me."

"Help!" came a cry from inside the room.

"Quick! Open it!" said Zan. She pulled on the knob while he tried to pull out the daggers that were stuck sideways in the door panel.

"Hey, is that you guys?" asked a friendly voice.

"Yes, we're trying to open the door," said Zan.

"Please hurry! The flames are getting closer," she called.

"On it," said Zan.

Owen managed to pull out one of the daggers, but there were several more jammed in the door. Zan helped him pull out the others.

One by one the daggers clunked onto the ground. Every now and then the doorknob would rattle as Charlie tried to get it open.

Finally, the last dagger dropped to the ground. Charlie flung open the door and nearly knocked over the others.

Together, they raced for the stairwell.

"You set the school on fire?" asked Owen.

She nodded.

"Impressive," he responded.

The teens raced out of the school and into the parking lot. There, Principal Allan waited.

"So you tricked Tonia into giving up her zleader status," said Zan.

"Oh, she just wanted to lead a normal life," said Allan. "Zleaders are chosen. They don't have a choice."

Charlie walked closer to him, examining his eyes. "But your eyes aren't glowing green. Or you're wearing contact lenses?" she asked.

He shook his head. "I'm not the zleader," he said. "But good job in pouring salt around the school. You could have kept me here if I was the zleader."

"You gave our addresses to Tonia, didn't you?" accused Zan.

"That I did do," he admitted.

Zan was angry. "I'd kill you, but I have a rule that I don't kill humans," she said.

Suddenly, Principal Allan dropped to the ground.

"I don't have that rule," said Steve, standing right behind him. He held a bloody knife in his hand.

"Oh shit," said Owen, quickly dropping to the ground to check on Principal Allan. "I think he's still alive."

Charlie pulled out her dagger. She could see that Steve had glowing green eyes. "So she made you the zleader before she died. You lied to us," she said accusingly.

"That's right," he said. He came at her with the knife.

Zan quickly pulled the dagger out of her pocket.

Charlie struck with her dagger. She cut his arm. She was pleased to see that it didn't immediately heal up. That meant that he wasn't under the same protection that Tonia had been under. Though that could certainly change.

Zan lifted her leg and kicked at his arm, knocking the knife from it. "Hah!" she said. "You guys should really pick zleaders who know what they're doing. Picking someone off the streets is useless. That's why most zleaders don't last more than a few weeks."

Steve started running, but then seemed to hit an invisible barrier. He bounced back and fell onto the ground.

"Hey, cool," said Owen. "It worked."

Steve was on the ground, trying to pick

himself up. Charlie pushed her hand against his shoulder and he fell back on the ground.

The other two students surrounded him.

"Just do it!" he said. "I have nothing to live for. Tonia is gone permanently now." He pushed himself up from the ground, and then stood up.

"I'm getting really tired of this," said Charlie. "It's been nonstop zombies for me the past two years. Enough is enough! This has to end now."

She took her regular dagger and plunged it into his head. He dropped to the ground, dead.

"Umm, wait a minute," said Zan. "I thought he was the zleader? But, he's dead."

"Dammit!" said Charlie. She kicked the body. "What is going on here? Who the heck is the zleader? First, I think it's Tonia, but then no, it's supposed to be Principal Allan. But no, then it's supposed to be Steve. None of this makes sense."

"So the real issue here is that we have one smart zleader," said Owen.

"Yeah, like who is it?" asked Zan.

Charlie looked carefully at both of her friends. But there was no way it was either of them. They would have killed each other by now if it had been one of them.

"OK, friend inventory," said Zan. "Just who is left alive?"

"Let's see," said Charlie. "Who is left alive?"

"Well, for one, Stewart," said Owen.

"And Gran," said Charlie, reluctantly.

"And our families," added Zan.

"But they take no interest in what we do," said Owen in protest.

"OK, what about the rest of the teachers?"

Charlie shook her head. "It's not any of them."

"Students?" suggested Owen. "How about Ben, that guy from camp?"

"No, it's not him," said Zan. "He took off with his parents and went to California. A zleader would never go that far from their city."

Charlie's phone pinged. She lifted it up and looked at it.

"I think I might have some idea," she said.

They quickly hoofed it out of there as the school's fire alarms went off. The fire trucks arrived quickly and put the flames out. The team had already disposed of the bodies so there wouldn't be any embarrassing questions. Principal Allan was found alive, so the paramedics transported him to the hospital.

zzz

Later that night, the three of them met up.

"Is this a good idea?" asked Owen.

"Sure," Zan said. "There's a guy at the hardware store who said he's going to donate salt to anyone who wants to protect their house too."

"I've already done it for my house, and so has Zan," said Owen.

She nodded. "But why didn't we know about this sooner?"

"Because Stewart performed a spell to make the salt work," Charlie explained.

"Wait, is he a warlock or something?" asked Zan."

Charlie frowned. "I hope not. I think he just enjoys experimenting with the book. OK, Owen. I'm going to need you here. You need to help us sniff out the zleader."

"OK," he said. "I haven't done this

before though. While I'm good at getting my parents to confess they stole my candy, I'm not sure about finding a criminal."

"Well, just do your best," she said.

"OK," he replied.

Everyone got in Charlie's car and she drove to the movie theater. In downtown Portland, things were back to normal. Most people were oblivious that there was a zombie apocalypse. It was like things didn't affect you until you got swine flu, a bad injury, or someone broke into your home. Most people simply carried on with their normal lives until something happened to them.

They waited in front of the movie theater. Soon, Sara and Ce showed up.

"Hey, guys," said Ce. "Nice to see you again."

"Hi, everyone," said Sara. They all exchanged greetings and pleasantries.

"This movie is going to be so cool," said Ce.

Charlie looked at Owen. Owen was staring at Sara and Ce, puzzling things out.

"Say, you related to Tonia?" Owen asked Sara.

"Why, yes I am," she said. "Do you know

anything about her? She went missing after that school camping trip last week. Our parents are quite distraught."

"Nah," he said.

They went inside and paid for their tickets. Zan and Ce wanted popcorn and soda so they ordered from the food counter. Finally, they were seated in the theater.

Charlie wasn't able to sit beside Owen, so she texted him instead.

"Any idea?" she asked.

"Yep," he said. "It's Sara."

"What?" she said.

"Yep. These guys are good. They're learning to tone down the aggressiveness."

"OK, stay awake. I doubt they'll pull anything during the movie," she texted.

The film was excellent. There was plenty of action and just enough plot line so the viewer didn't get weary.

After the movie, they dropped their garbage into the trash can and then left the theater.

"Hey, guys. Let's take a shortcut down this alley," suggested Charlie.

"OK," said Ce, but Sara frowned.

"That was a good movie," Zan said to Owen. He nodded.

Charlie was walking beside Sara. She quickly pushed her up against the wall. She took her hand and brushed it over one of her eyes.

"Hey, what are you doing?" Sara asked.

A contact lens popped out of her eye. Beneath, her eye glowed green. Charlie pushed her onto the ground, yanking her enchanted dagger out of the pocket inside her jacket. She quickly plunged it into her head and recited the spell, "Reliqua autem impius!"

"Nooo, what are you doing?" screamed Ce.

It didn't take long. Sara struggled for a bit, but then quickly died.

Not long after, Ce crumpled to the ground.

"Good," said Zan.

"That should take care of any followers," said Owen.

They quickly hid the bodies in the nearest blue dumpster.

As they walked back to Charlie's car, Owen asked a question.

"Say, do all the zombies die when you kill a zleader?"

"Pretty much," she said.

"So, is that it then?" asked Zan.
She nodded.

zzz

"Good work, Charlie!" said Stewart at the beginning of bio class.

"Well, it was a lot of running back and forth. So many zleaders, it was crazy."

"I've informed the Portland Police that the zombie plague is done. The city is now safe again."

"That's great," she said. "I guess that means I can retire now." She went to take a seat at the back of class. It was now October. She'd been at Portland High School for a month now. It felt like it had been a whole year.

Owen took a seat beside her.

"Hey, you want to hang out on the weekend?" he asked.

She shook her head to the negative. "No offense. I just need to stay away from anything and everything having to do with zombies."

"That's OK. I understand."

"Did Zan say yes to the dance?"

He nodded. "We're only going as friends though. That's fine with me."

She smiled at him, pleased. It was great to have male friends who didn't want anything from their female friends. People should be allowed to fall in love naturally, without wanting anything in return.

Zan entered the classroom and waved.

"When is this dance anyway?" she asked.

"Later in the month, for Halloween," he replied.

She nodded. "Well, maybe I'll go alone," she said.

"That's cool. Or we can just all go as friends."

She smiled. "As long as there are no zombie costumes," she said.

"Well, I heard that zombies are popular this year, so I'm sure there will be at least a few of them. Think you can handle it?"

She pondered the thought. "As long as no one dresses up as a spider, I should be fine."

The rest of the day was uneventful.

Charlie went home and planned her costume. She decided to go as a zombie slayer, mostly because she really didn't have the garb for anything else. She knew Stewart would frown upon it, but this was the one day each year that she could go as who she wanted, and she could truly be herself.

zzz

Not much happened over the next week or so. It was a relief to have a break and focus on schoolwork for a change. Somehow she managed to pass her exams with all As and Bs, despite her mind not totally being there. All she could think about were zombies and more zombies. She wasn't certain if the solution was to talk about it to her mentor or her friends, or to see a psychologist. But since there were so many zombie deniers, perhaps going the pro route was a bad idea.

The school still had a lingering smell of smoke. They were talking about renovating the basement and turning it into classrooms, since even the unburned section was so smoky.

Her phone rang. It was Owen.

"Hi, Owen! What's up?" she asked.

"Hi," he said. "Listen, I was thinking, maybe I could start a business."

"That's a great idea. You should not become a zlayer," she suggested. "It's not as fun as you think. So, what's your business idea?" she asked.

"I was thinking that I could run a body disposal service."

"What the?"

"You know, like we had to do. Except you can call someone."

There was silence.

A roar of laughter escaped from the other end of the phone.

She laughed. "You got me. You're so funny!"

"Yeah, fortunately there are no more zombies so no one would need that service."

"See you in school tomorrow," she said before hanging up. "Sheesh. Some people!"

She finished up her schoolwork, and then did her chores. It helped Gran out. She was just finishing up her chores when her phone pinged. She picked it up. It was from Stewart.

"In trouble. Need help," the message read.

She sighed. "Where R U?" she typed.

"Ivywood Mansion in the basement."

"B there in 10."

"Hey, Gran. I'm going to Ivywood Mansion. Stewart is locked up in the dungeon there for some reason or other."

"OK, dear. Have fun," she said. "Don't stay up too late."

She smiled. Gran was so understanding. She threw off her pajamas and put real clothes on. She grabbed her backpack and filled it up with supplies.

Under the underwear in her drawer, she saw the daggers. Naturally she'd always have her basic dagger on hand for self-defense, but what about the titanium one? It seemed fine. It wasn't damaged in any way.

She didn't really need it, did she? There were no more zombies left. Chances were that Stewart got mixed up with some thugs, as often he needed underground information.

Her phone pinged again. "Bring the t dagger," the message said.

"Bring the what? Oh, the titanium dagger. Great."

She slung the dagger and its holster around her body, and then put her jacket on. It was time to go.

CHAPTER 16

She drove her car north to Ivywood
Mansion. This was an old Victorian mansion
owned by the city. It had fallen into
disrepair. The family had tried to save it but
didn't have the money. Eventually, the city
had purchased the mansion and the
surrounding acreage from the family, which
made everyone happy. This meant that the
city would restore it and treat it as a historic
site, preventing developers from getting
their hands on it.

She hadn't seen the mansion before and
was amazed as she drove up the hill. She
couldn't see all of it, as it was starting to get
dark out, but it seemed to be in way better
condition than many of the other old houses
she'd seen over the years. The property it
was on was vast. She knew that there were
many weddings, dances, and special events

held here over the years. The house was also considered a museum and open to the public at certain times.

She parked her car and headed inside. The front door was unlocked. She walked into the vestibule where it said to clean your shoes before entering. She ignored the sign. She walked through into the main entrance.

How odd. There should be an alarm or something, but no bells went off. Stewart said he was locked up in the basement, so she headed down the stairs. There might be an old wooden service elevator that ran on cables in the back, but she wasn't about to waste time to look for it. She walked down two sets of stairs until she reached the basement.

She was in a narrow hallway with doors on each side. Many of those doors had signs hanging that read, NOT OPEN TO THE PUBLIC. A few were bathrooms for the guests.

She walked down the hallway, trying to figure out where Stewart was being held. So far, she had not seen anyone else. When she strained her ears, she could almost hear a faint sound of classical or orchestral music, kind of like from a scratchy, old record. It was possible. There could be a caretaker on site.

She'd better speed things up just in case a security guard was making the rounds. She didn't want to get caught.

At the end of the hallway, there was a door. She tried the knob, but it was locked. This would be simple. It had an older style of lock that was easily picked. She quickly opened the door. Ahead of her was a set of old wooden stairs. A damp smell of mildew spewed up into her face. Brushing the air in front of her, she descended the staircase. At the bottom was a small jail cell, enclosed with steel bars.

"Finally!" said Stewart. "You took long enough."

"It's been ten minutes," she said.

"Look out!" he said, but it was too late. Someone hit her over the head. She collapsed to the ground, slowly losing consciousness.

"Don't hurt her!" said Stewart. The small dungeon door was opened up and she was deposited inside.

She woke up a few minutes later.

"You OK?" Stewart asked.

"What's going on?" she asked. "Are there

zombies here?"

"Well, you're not going to believe it," said Stewart. "But I'm actually excited for the events ahead."

"Why are you here anyway?" she asked.

"I got a telephone call saying they had some old books from the Victorian era that I might be interested in. I was to meet them here. But when I got here and went to the front door, four people grabbed me, then dragged me down to the basement and tossed me in here."

"Did you see any zombies when they took you through the house?" she asked.

"No, but it's not like I was able to closely look at anyone."

"So you never got to see any books?" she asked.

He smiled. "Nope."

She wandered around the small jail cell, testing the bars. Some were rusted and stained, but they held well. The floor of the cell was dark concrete. It filled most of the small room, with three walls also made of concrete. There appeared to be no escape, except through the main barred door.

"Forget it," said Stewart. "I already had a look around."

"Well, you forget about my famous lock-picking skills," she said.

"Yeah, but they took your backpack away from you." He nodded to just outside the cage.

"Oh, I don't need that," she said. She touched the brooch she wore on her top. She unhooked it and took the pin off. She walked up to the door. "OK, I'm going to have to do this backwards," she said.

"Good luck," said Stewart.

"It's all right," she replied. "This was all part of that lock-picking class I took." She stood as close to the door as she could. She reached around with her left hand to feel for the keyhole where the key would fit in. She found it. She held the brooch carefully in her right hand. She drew it around to the front. She slid the brooch deep down into the keyhole and pressed.

The lock clicked. It was a simple lock. She carefully drew out her brooch and put it back on her top. She pressed the door of the cage and it popped open.

"Nice work," said Stewart. "Now let's get out of here."

Charlie grabbed her backpack that was dumped on the floor. She slipped it on over her shoulders, just in case she'd have to fight. She found the dagger that had been in her back pocket, which they had removed, and put it back. She still had the special titanium dagger under her jacket. They hadn't found that one. That was actually a good thing, as she didn't want to lose that one. It would be much harder to replace, and Stewart would be mad at her if she lost it.

The pair climbed the rickety staircase to the basement and headed back into the small hallway. There was no one around them. They walked quickly and quietly to the main stairs.

While they were heading up the stairs to the main floor, they started to hear music. It was the same classical, mostly orchestral music, and sounded like it was being played on a gramophone, complete with skips and scratches.

"I think the sound is coming from above," Stewart said. "Let's go find out."

"Sure," Charlie said, patting her dagger. "There has to be a reasonable explanation as to why they lured you here."

"Well, most likely to lure you here too," he said, tucking in his blue shirt and smoothing his hair.

"Ooh, you don't think this is related to zombies, do you?"

He looked at her. "Why else are we even here?" he replied.

Most likely Tonia had gotten word that Stewart had been asking questions around town about zombies. Stewart didn't like to impede any other types of crime in the city, as he felt it wasn't his job. While zrug was a concern, he was more concerned with crimes such as zombies eating, killing, or turning humans.

By now, they were on one of the upper floors. This must be where the family's bedrooms had been. The doors were large and framed with a richly coated dark brown lacquer. Each door had a tarnished brass keyhole and doorknob.

They walked down the hallway to the end. No one was here. At the end of the hallway was a smaller flight of stairs, supposedly the one that the staff would have used. They walked up to it and ascended.

As they walked up, the sound of the music became louder. They didn't bother being quiet with their footsteps, as the music filled the corridor. Soon they were at the top of the staircase. Ahead of them was a door. Charlie opened it and beckoned Stewart through.

Ahead appeared to be some sort of festival. She closed the door. She and Stewart slowly crept down the hallway. Up ahead was a party of some sort. The lights were low. On one side was a dance party, with people twirling around to the music. There wasn't a lot of coordination here. They just did their own thing. To the left was a long table full of food and drinks. The other half of the attendees stood there, chatting.

A putrid scent filled the room. Charlie ignored it, while Stewart tried to cover his nose with his handkerchief.

As they crept closer, they realized something was amiss. The people dancing on the floor were actually zombies. They were not only in various stages of decay, but also in various stages of undress. The people to the side were zombies too.

She watched as one of them drank a glass of wine, but the red liquid came out through their stomach. She looked down at the floor. It wasn't very clean.

"I wonder if they turned after they came

here for the party?" asked Stewart.

"Probably," she said. "Otherwise, I think it'd be difficult to get all of them here."

Their voices must have attracted their attention. Every single zombie in the place turned and looked in their direction.

"Oh crap," said Charlie.

"Hey, look everyone," said one of the zombies. He must have been the lead guy, as he was the least decomposed of them all. "Dinner has arrived!" The other zombies laughed, while some simply groaned.

"I think we should run," said Stewart. They both took off, bolting for the exit door, but soon discovered that it was already blocked by a zombie.

CHAPTER 17

This zombie was strong. It must have been newly turned too. It grabbed each of their arms and dragged them back to the party. Charlie scrambled for her weapon while Stewart wondered why he hadn't brought his dagger in from his car.

The zombie dragged them back to the leader. Stewart leaned in and punched him in the face. The guy behind them let them go. She brought out her dagger and plunged it into his head. He went down.

Then they felt themselves being pulled to the side. In seconds, they were chained to the wall.

"Help!" Charlie cried. Stewart was chained beside her.

They looked up and saw what appeared to be a wedding couple. She was still dressed in a long white gown with satin and lace, while the groom was dressed in a black tuxedo. The pair danced around the room. Some of the zombies were seated and didn't appear like they would ever be standing up again.

"I wonder how long this party has been going on?" asked Stewart.

"Ugh, how do we get out of here?" she asked.

"Do your lock-picking trick again," he suggested.

"Errr," she said.

For the moment, they were largely ignored. A zombie, who was likely the emcee, stood up front and was making unintelligible sounds. But somehow the other zombies understood him, as they laughed, or made what sounded like laughing sounds.

A zombie walked in front of them, dragging her legs. She was wearing a dress, and had a large protrusion coming from her lower abdomen.

"Say, that female zombie looks pregnant," said Charlie.

"Yikes," said Stewart. "That's not something you see every day."

"That's sad," said Charlie. "Whoever bit her should be ashamed of themselves."

The next few minutes were fairly uneventful. The zombies didn't do much but moan and groan, and drag themselves around the party room.

While they partied, she used her teeth to drag her top closer to her mouth. Then she used her tongue to unlatch the brooch. She then carefully wrapped her teeth around it and slid it out of the fabric.

Now that she had the brooch securely in her mouth, she carefully turned left to insert the pin into the cuff on her left hand. Fortunately, the cuffs and chains weren't installed too far apart on the wall. Once she had her hand free, she did the other side. The zombies weren't paying attention. She quickly did her feet.

"Quickly," said Stewart.

"Hey, what is dinner doing?" asked one of the zombies. He dragged his feet over. "They are trying to escape!" he said accusingly.

The other zombie faces turned to look at them.

"I think it's dinnertime!" he cried. With his jaw chomping up and down, he moved toward Stewart.

Charlie quickly undid the cuff that held

Stewart's right leg, and then undid the left one. It was the best she could do.

Just as the zombie leaned into his neck, there was a cry from the other side of the room. Everyone glanced in that direction.

The pregnant zombie woman collapsed to the floor. She started screaming, her hands on her lower abdomen.

"Oh no," said Charlie. "It's not what I think is happening, is it?"

"It is," said Stewart.

The zombie that had been about to have him for dinner lost interest. He walked over to where the woman was lying on the floor.

Charlie quickly undid one arm cuff and then the other. Stewart's chains dropped to the floor. "Thanks! That was close!"

They could have hightailed it out of there right then, but they were as fascinated by the turn of events as the rest of the zombies were. They watched as the zombie woman took a deep breath and then bore down. It didn't take long. A small zombie child popped out from under her dress. It was gray and covered in blood and gore.

"It's a small blessing," said Stewart. "It's dead."

Charlie sighed. "Whew. That would be

horrific if there were zombie babies."

A few zombies lost interest and came their way.

Charlie yanked her dagger out of her back pocket and handed it to Stewart. He used it to dispatch some of the zombies nearest to them.

"Let's clear the rest of the room!" he cried.

She tossed her backpack on the floor and pulled out another dagger. They did the perimeter of the room first, boxing the remaining zombies in. They left the stagnant zombies alone for the moment. They weren't hurting anyone. They simply sat in their chairs, grimacing at each other.

"Look behind you!" she cried at Stewart.

The emcee grabbed at his arms, but Stewart struck fast. The zombie went down.

With great pleasure, Charlie was able to kill the zombie that had been about to eat her mentor. He went down fast.

By now, blood and gore covered both student and mentor. Usually zombie fighting didn't get this gory. But the good news was that it wasn't like in the movies. If you got splashed with infected blood, you didn't turn. As soon as a zombie was dead, their remains had little effect on the living, other than grossing people out.

The gore didn't bother Charlie or Stewart. They were both used to it.

Soon, the last remaining zombies were those seated in chairs around the room, and also the zombie woman, who had just given birth, was still lying on the floor.

"You go check the rest of the floor," said Stewart. "I'll finish up here."

She nodded, and headed down the hallway on the other side. She peered into the rooms. They had some interesting displays here, things that looked like Gran's china or silverware. But she didn't see any more zombies. She decided to head back to the party room.

"There, that's done," said Stewart.

"Great," she said. "Now it's cleanup time."

They did their best to clear the room of bodies by putting them in the dumpsters outside the building. They also did their best to mop up the mess on the floors. They didn't bother with the party decorations, food, or drink. They'd leave that to whatever staff was still alive and would be arriving for their shifts the next day.

"OK, all good," said Charlie.

Stewart looked down at himself. "I think we should clean ourselves up a bit, just in case we run into any civilians outside."

She nodded.

They headed to the men's and women's bathrooms.

Charlie discarded all of her clothing, placing them in a sealed plastic bag. She washed off with soap and water as best she could. She put on clean clothes from her backbag. Then she met Stewart back in the hallway.

"I've trashed the computer that had the security footage on it." He held up a black USB drive, and then tucked it into his pocket.

"What happened here?" she asked.

He shrugged. "A zombie must have gotten in somehow and disturbed the wedding festivities."

"I don't want to be the one who explains what happened to an entire family," she said.

"There are going to be an awful lot of bodies ending up in the Oregon landfill," commented Stewart. Then they both burst out laughing.

"So, did someone just show up at the

door?"

"Maybe. Probably a guest. They must have been attacked somewhere, or perhaps even on the property."

The team was done here, so they left the mansion. They spent the next hour touring the estate but didn't see any other zombies around. It was possible that the first zombie had been bitten outside the property, even at home.

"There's not much more we can do here," he said. "We should head for home and get some rest."

"But I don't get it," said Charlie. "Killing the zleaders would have killed any other zombies, right? Why are any left?"

He frowned. "There is only one explanation for it."

"Which is?" she asked, walking with him to their cars.

"That a new zleader has moved into town."

"What? Again?" she exclaimed. "You mean that another zleader leaves their own city and moves here so soon after we killed the previous one?"

"Well, it's rare, but it does happen when that city has been destroyed," he said.

"That's bizarre," she said, getting back in her own car.

"Don't worry too much. We'll figure it out, OK? Be safe getting home," he said, getting into his car.

"Yeah, you too," she replied.

They each drove for a while, thinking on their own.

Charlie called Stewart on the drive home. "There are so many rules that sometimes I can't digest it all," she said.

"I know. You'll soon get the hang of things. You've only been doing this for less than two years now. And it's really unusual for this to happen."

"It's bugging me. I wonder which town got destroyed?" she asked.

He turned on the news. She could hear his radio through the phone.

"Moodville has suffered a bad wildfire that has destroyed much of the town," said the radio announcer.

Stewart turned off the news. "That's the answer right there."

"Wow," said Charlie. "Perhaps we should enlist the aid of that town to help us out here."

He laughed. Soon they were both back at

their homes. "OK, so take it easy for a bit. I'm going to listen to the news to see if I can learn more."

She yawned. "OK, good night then."

Charlie flopped down in her bed, exhausted. She couldn't believe that they had to deal with another zombie infestation. She hadn't known that if they lost their home that they'd just move in on another one. That was crazy, but she guessed it made sense. She quickly fell asleep.

She dreamt that she was in Hawaii, sipping a piña colada. She wore her tiniest bikini and looked great in it. She didn't even have scar lines or anything. The weather was hot and dry, instead of being cold and humid. The people surrounding her were friendly and young, not decayed and rotting.

She lifted her drink to take a sip, and then noticed there was a finger floating in it. She forced herself awake.

"Stupid brain!" she said, chastising herself. "I can't even have a nice dream to myself." Soon, she fell back asleep again.

zzz

The next day it was back to school, as per usual. Everyone was getting excited about the Halloween dance coming up at the end of the month. There was a committee for decorations, one for food and drink, and one for entertainment. She steered clear of that but did purchase a dance ticket.

"You know, we're going to have to figure out how to smuggle booze into this event," said Zan.

"I've seen these steel bracelet flasks you can get to keep your booze in," said Owen.

"Nah, not enough volume," said Zan.

"What were you up to the other night?" asked Owen.

"Oh, we had to go fight zombies at the Ivywood Mansion," explained Charlie.

"What? I thought they were done," he said in protest.

"That's what I thought," said Charlie.

"Nah, there are always zombies. They're all over the country," said Zan.

"Really?" asked Charlie.

"Yep. Usually they keep a low profile though. But most of those murders you hear about likely have something to do with zombies."

"That's crazy," said Charlie. "How can we stop them?"

"Just keep at it," said Zan, patting her jacket where she kept her dagger.

"But I thought when a zleader was killed, that it killed all of their own zombies too?" asked Owen, puzzled.

"That does happen. Trouble is that the last person a zombie has bitten then turns into a zleader after the original zleader is killed. Sure, all the other zombies die, except for the last one."

"Yes, but all the Portland zombies were killed off. The ones we'll see now are from Moodville, apparently."

Zan frowned. "That's right. They had an incident there," she recalled.

"Yeah, a zombie from Moodville must have survived, and headed to Ivywood Mansion." Charlie thought about it a bit, recalling the previous night's events. "But, we didn't kill a zleader, so they must have been long gone by the time we arrived."

"Great," said Owen. "Another zleader out there."

"Well," said Charlie. "The good news is that you can help me in finding this new one."

"Cool," he said, nodding. "Things were getting boring around here anyway."

The team laughed.

CHAPTER 18

A week passed, giving the team a break. There weren't too many incidents in the news that could involve zombies. The good news was that this gang was smarter and keeping a lower profile. The bad news was that this z-gang was probably a lot smarter.

Charlie kept busy with schoolwork. She envied Owen and his part-time job to earn extra cash for his family. Not because he had extra cash, but because he had something else to occupy his mind.

During her time off, she practiced her moves in the backyard. She also liked to up the game and think up new surprises. She could now run up a wall halfway, then flip around, and land on the ground. But the trouble with that move was that it took a few seconds, when a zombie could strike in a split second. She had a few scars on her body, but most of those were acquired from training. She had trained in martial arts and had a few katana scars on her body from the dojo in Dallas.

She practiced climbing up into a tree and doing surveillance of the neighborhood. Everything was quiet.

She jumped back down and headed indoors.

"Here's your phone, dear," said Gran. "It's been ringing off the hook." She took the phone from her.

"Hello?" she said.

"We have a problem," said Stewart on the other end.

"Of course we do. You never call me for any other reason," she responded.

"There is a fashion show at the local community theater. Word is that there will be zombies as models."

She was silent for a bit. "Wow, just when I thought I'd heard everything."

"I know," he said. He gave her the address, and then hung up.

"Need your help," she texted Zan. She decided to leave Owen alone. He wouldn't be interested in a fashion show anyway.

Charlie picked up Zan from her house.

"How are things going?"

"Good," she said. "It's nice to have a break for a change. I might actually be looking forward to Halloween monsters."

"Me too," said Charlie. "There should be a happy medium between zombie fighting or quiet, but it's either one or the other all at once."

Zan nodded knowingly. "So, what's up with this fashion show?" she asked.

"Well, it's a local designer's show. Apparently, he's advertising that the models he's using are zombies."

"Weird. Maybe it's just a marketing ploy?" She was busy looking at her smartphone.

"Not sure," said Charlie. "Stewart was creeped out enough that he passed the details, and a pair of tickets, to us."

"Good," she said. "The designer is called Larry Zombie," she read from her smartphone. She thought a bit. "Say, is it possible that Larry is a zombie?"

Charlie shook her head. "Nah. Zombies don't have jobs. Remember how Tonia dropped out of school. They can't stick to a routine."

"Right," said Zan. "Well, let's go and see what this thing is about."

They arrived at the local community theater and found a parking spot. Charlie used her Parking Kitty app to pay for the parking. The amount of money she spent on parking in the city was crazy. It was a good thing the app offered a frequent user discount.

They both left the car and headed to the entrance. There was a line, so they got in the back to wait.

Everyone in line looked fairly normal. There was the usual share of brightly colored hair, piercings, and torn clothing, but no one looked like a zombie.

Finally, they were allowed inside the theater. Charlie had a quick look at the concession stand workers, but they looked normal too. They found their seats. There were a few people moving things around on stage, but nothing unusual was happening.

Zan sniffed the air. "It has a weird smell to it. Like rotting flesh."

"Well, it could just be someone's sandwich is off," Charlie commented.

Finally, it was time for the fashion show to begin. It started off with the emcee announcing Larry Zombie, and then having him present a short speech on what his collection was about. Then, it was time for the show.

The lights dimmed and the music started. It was an instrumental. The curtains slowly opened. Bright LED lights flashed spots of different prime colors, but red was the main one.

The first model walked onto the stage. Charlie moved her head closer.

"It's just someone dressed up as a zombie," whispered Zan.

She nodded back.

The next 20 models on stage were the same. Their face and body makeup was amazing, but would still never fool experts like Zan and Charlie.

"Can we just go now?" asked Zan. "Or should we hang out for a bit?"

Charlie shook her head. "No, something's up. I can smell it."

The curtain closed for a bit. Then it was time for the finale. The curtains opened back up. The lights in the place went out. Then, the LED lights started flashing and rotating. The spotlight turned on center stage.

In the front was a figure, hunched over. It was wearing a bright yellow jumpsuit with polka dots. In front of it was a human, holding a leash in its hand. The human moved forward. The zombie followed behind. The audience raised a collective "ahhhh."

"Good makeup," said someone in the audience.

"Nice clothes," said another voice.

As the zombie act walked down the platform, another zombie and her master appeared on the stage. The human walked confidently ahead, pulling the leash of the zombie behind her. The zombie suddenly rushed forward, arms ahead. The master had a stick in her hand and beat at the zombie to keep it back. The zombie relented and slowed down.

The first pair had reached the end of the platform near the opposite wall. There, they waited. Several more zombies and their masters entered the stage and walked down the runway.

Finally, the last of them were at the end of the walkway. And then the lights went completely out. Everyone waited expectantly. But then the screaming started.

"What's happening?" cried Zan.

"Not sure," said Charlie, digging out her

cell phone. She flipped it open and held it up in the air. "Bad news. They let the zombies off of their leashes."

"Really?" said Zan, jumping into action. She had her dagger out in a second. Charlie pulled hers out too.

"So, where are they?"

"They've made it into the crowd."

"Why would they do that?" asked Zan "Is it some form of human mind control?"

"Ask questions later," said Charlie, leaping at a zombie ahead of her. The zombie was soon struck down.

"How many do you think?" asked Zan, stabbing the nearest zombie in the head.

"I think I counted ten. So, we're down to eight now."

By now, many of the attendees had scattered in the theater. Some had managed to make their way into the lobby, and then outside.

A few stupid ones simply stood there, thinking it was all a big joke. They watched as the zombies bit some of their fellow human beings, while other zombies came out of the darkness, knocked them over, and started chewing on their necks. Charlie just shook her head. There were still so many people who believed that zombies were a conspiracy theory, rather than real. Yet, the evidence was here right in front of them.

"Now it's six," Zan said. But then, as their eyes adjusted to the darkness, they watched as four humans, who had been bitten, now turned. Their skin was gray, and their eyes glowed green. "Back to ten," she said.

"We have to get as many as we can," yelled Charlie. She leapt forward and immediately took down the four newer ones. They were a lot easier to kill than the already established ones.

"I can't open the doors," screamed a human in the distance. "They're locked!"

"Crap," said Charlie. "Whoever did this to us has locked us in!"

"No time for that," said Zan. "We have to kill as many as we can. We can't let them leave."

But as fast as Zan and Charlie leapt at the zombies, cutting them down, there seemed to be more created. Soon the entire room smelled of rotting blood. The event was a monumental disaster and the body count continued to rise.

Finally, there was a reprieve. There were

only so many victims left. She breathed a sigh of relief. It could have been worse. Fortunately, the smarter people had left.

"Hey, let's check the stage," said Zan. "Some might have gotten out that way."

"OK," said Charlie, following behind. "We'll come back and do cleanup shortly."

They pulled themselves up onto the stage. It looked clear, but they had to check. It appeared that this space backstage was small. There was a tiny changing room off to the side, but no one in it. Then they heard a scrambling sound. Charlie turned around.

"It's OK. I've got him," said Zan. She was behind Larry Zombie, holding a dagger at his neck.

"Hey, take it easy," he said. "I'm not one of them."

Charlie stormed up to him. "Why did you do it?" asked Charlie. "It's a mess out there. Why would you release real, live zombies into the audience?"

"I didn't know," cried Larry. "Some guy called John said they were actors, ready for some performance art. But he told us to be careful around their jaws, as they really liked to get into their roles."

"But, whose idea was it to let them

loose?" asked Charlie.

"It was John's. He said it'd be a part of the performance art of the show. But he didn't say anything about them being real, or them running around eating or killing people."

"Zan, let him go." She released the designer.

"So, it was a John who did this?" she asked.

"Yes."

"Did he look like a drug dealer? Because I know a guy who has been involved in zombie business before," Charlie said.

"Yeah, that could be him," said Larry. "He looked kind of stoned."

"So did he approach you first?' asked Zan.

Larry nodded. "I was just going to dress up the models and apply makeup. You can see some of the posters we have around the theatre. It was after these were done that he showed up at my shop, saying he had a fabulous idea."

Charlie grimaced. "So, what did this cost you?"

"Nothing," said Larry. "He told me these guys were theater students, brand new actors. They wanted to learn so they wouldn't be charging any fees, at least this time around."

She nodded. "Well, thank you for your time." The girls turned to go.

"Hey, I'm so sorry this happened," said Larry. "It was not my intention."

"Nope," said Zan. "I suggest you start cleaning up this mess, unless you want to lose your rental deposit from the theater."

She and Charlie walked to the stage and hopped down. They did a quick tour around the theater, but everyone was dead. If in doubt, Zan used her dagger.

They went to the doors, but they were locked, just like before.

Charlie soon had the lock picked. They entered the lobby, but there was no one around. Then they heard sirens in the distance.

"I wonder what the purpose of this was," said Zan.

"Well, isn't it obvious," she said, as she led the way to her car. "Someone is trying to start a zombie uprising. It's a lot easier to do it in an enclosed space than to send a zombie out at random on the streets."

Zan gave a wry smile. "That's crazy.

People need to stay home or something."

"Well, you got that right. Somehow this city isn't safe anymore." Charlie clicked the button on her keys. The doors unlocked. They got inside and left. "It looks like we're going to have to visit John again, but let's do it after we get washed up and the police have left," she suggested.

"Right. Maybe we can do it tomorrow night? I doubt the drug dealers are going to be attempting anything else tonight."

"This will also give us an opportunity to find out where the zombies came from. They may actually lead us to the zleader," suggested Charlie.

They headed for home. Once there, Charlie had to fill Stewart in. He was glad that they had followed up, otherwise, the situation could have been far worse.

CHAPTER 19

Charlie and Zan had no luck finding John or Stan. The guys had left town. Resigned, they decided to lay low. The good news was that it was the Halloween dance that night. They were at Charlie's house getting ready.

Gran had trimmed Charlie's hair and was using the curling iron.

"This brings me back to the olden days," mused Gran.

"Her hair looks great," said Zan. "I'm next."

Both the girls had decided to go as zombie slayers, which meant they could bring their daggers and no one at school would bat an eye.

"I heard that Principal Allan is back at school," said Zan.

"Is he now? We'll have to keep an eye on him."

"Too bad we didn't turn him over to the police," said Zan.

"Yeah. Well, we both thought he was dead." She shrugged. "I'm over it. Hopefully, he's learned his lesson. If not, next time we'll teach him one."

"Yep, we'll have all of our gear for tonight. Just in case there is another zombie incident."

"Yep, I could get used to this," said Charlie. "It's almost like each day I get out of bed in the morning, expecting a new fight. I wonder if I could really retire. Take a break."

"Don't know," said Zan. "I've never wanted to retire. Life is so dull without the zombie fighting."

Charlie's grimace turned into a smile. "You know, you're right. That's a positive way to think about it."

Soon Gran had finished with their hair. They applied their makeup. They decided to add some bright red makeup to simulate blood splotches. They smeared some on their clothing. Each painted the ends of their daggers in dark red.

"OK, Gran is going to drop us off, which means we can sip some vodka from our flasks if we want while at the party."

"Cool, did you tell her that?" asked Zan, tucking a black curl behind her shoulder.

"Yep, she knows me well," said Charlie.

Gran was waiting for them. "Both you girls look like fabulous zlayers. Let's hope there are no zombies at the party. You both deserve a break."

They both smiled at her.

Along the way, they picked up Owen. He was dressed up as a zombie.

Both girls frowned.

"But what else would I dress up as?" he asked. "I'm between two zlayers."

They all laughed.

Soon Gran had them at the high school. She drove around to the back and let them off near the gym where the dance was being held.

"Just call me when you're done," she said.

"Yes, we will," said Charlie, exiting the vehicle. She followed after Zan and Owen, who were already at the door.

"This is going to be fun," said Owen. "What could possibly go wrong on dance night?"

Charlie had a good laugh. "Well, we haven't fought any zombies at the school for a bit, and certainly not at a dance."

zzz

The friends headed into the gym, handing their tickets to the people manning the table at the front. Inside, the gym was about half full.

"I hope more people show," said Zan, disappointed.

"Relax," said Owen. "The party is just starting. I'll get us some drinks." He headed over to the beverage table.

Charlie and Zan made their way out into the crowd, critiquing and gossiping about people's costumes. There was a fair share of vampires, pumpkins, ghosts, and superheroes.

"Hey, I don't see anyone else dressed up as zombies or zombie slayers," Zan commented.

Charlie smiled. "Good, we aced it then."

"So, do you think there are any zombies here?" she asked.

"Don't know. Hey, thanks for the drinks, Owen." It was too early to add vodka, so they sipped their drinks and enjoyed the music and costumes.

Much of the music was from the 80s, lively and upbeat. She encouraged Zan and Owen to hit the dance floor. She took some pictures of them with her cell phone.

"Enjoying the dance?" asked Stewart.

"Oh, hey, Stew…I mean Mr. George. Why yes, I am. Too bad you got stuck with teacher duty."

"Oh, I don't mind," he said. "I'll keep an eye on things to ensure that nothing goes wrong."

"It seems fairly quiet," she said. "I expect more students will arrive later. So, any more leads?" she asked. Might as well ask now so that she didn't have to call or text him later.

"None," he said. "Unless John and Stan come back to the city."

Zan and Owen were done with their dance and came back to her. Stewart waved and then went back to chatting with the other teachers.

By now, more people drifted into the gym so the dance songs picked up the pace. It was now time to add the vodka to their punch. Owen got them more drinks. They drank half, and then Zan and Charlie used their flasks to fill up the cups.

Once they had their alcohol, they smiled more often and all headed onto the dance floor to pick up the beat.

zzz

It was nearly time for the close of the dance. Nothing unusual had happened. The teens had a great time at the party. Some slipped outside to have a smoke, or to drink. A few cuddled with their boyfriends or girlfriends. The drink table ran out of chips and punch, but they had already worked their way completely through the flasks.

Zan stumbled a bit as they crossed the room.

"Hey, be careful there," Owen said.

"Well, I think it's time I call Gran to pick us up," said Charlie, slurring her words. She pulled her cell phone out of her pocket. "It's time," she texted.

"Be right there," Gran texted back.

"We should go meet her out front," said Charlie. The three of them headed out to the main door. They were about to leave when they heard loud screams coming from the back of the gym.

zzz

The three friends removed their daggers from their clothing and raced to the back. There were many screams and cries. Some students fled the gym. The teachers moved in, trying to figure out what was happening.

"Wahhh," cried one of the female students, dressed up as a princess. "He bit me!"

Zan and Charlie looked at each other.

"This is it," Owen replied.

They told people to go home and that they'd handle it. At the very back were two zombies and the girl who was dressed up as a princess.

She held out her arm. It had indeed been bitten.

"Hey, someone get a first-aid kit," called out a teacher. Someone ran to get one.

"Are you all right?" asked Charlie warily.

She nodded. The two zombies just stood there.

"Hey, you a zombie," asked Zan, punching one in the arm. No response.

The girl was helped away to have her arm treated.

The lights in the gym were dimming. The music stopped and the disco lights turned off.

Charlie went to raise her dagger, but someone knocked it out of her hand.

"Look!" cried Zan. "They aren't zombies."

Charlie had a closer look. They were merely kids dressed up as zombies. But they were so stoned out of their minds that they just leaned against the wall.

"OK, so they just bit her?"

Zan shrugged. "I guess so."

"OK, let's get out of here," said Owen. "I'm done with tonight."

Charlie had a quick look at the girl as she headed out.

"False alarm," confirmed Stewart.

"OK, let me know if you hear of anything else."

Gran came, picked them up, and drove everyone home.

Charlie was looking forward to having a nice hot bath and then sleeping. The weekend would be spent doing homework.

They entered the house. "Nice evening, dear?" asked Gran, holding the door open for her.

"Yep," she said.

"Did everyone get pissed?" Gran asked.

"Gran!" she said in protest.

"Relax, dear. We did the same when I was a teen. As long as no one got hurt."

Charlie dumped her bag and jacket near the door. "No, it was fine. There was a false alarm, but nothing weird happened. I hope I can take a break this weekend."

She headed up to her room and collapsed.

ZZZ

Her phone pinged. She woke up and picked it up. "Good news, sort of," read the message. "I've tracked down John and Stan. They're back in town. Go to their place and find out what's going on."

"Great, I guess the weekend is gone," she said, getting out of bed. She quickly had a shower and got dressed. She grabbed a waffle on the way out the door. She got into her car, and then called Zan and Owen. Owen didn't answer, but Zan did.

"We have a lead," she said and then hung up.

Zan met her at the curb outside of her house.

"Where's Owen? I tried calling him."

"He has a hangover," Zan explained.

"Really? I didn't think he drank all that much."

Zan shrugged as the car left the driveway. "He must have a delicate constitution."

They drove to the drug dealers' residence. First, they drove past. Then they drove two blocks away and parked the car. Charlie used the Parking Kitty app to pay for parking. The pair hopped out of the vehicle and moved in.

"Do you have your weapons?" asked Charlie.

Zan nodded.

As they walked down the alley, there was a terrible stench about the place. They were both used to it, but just noted that it shouldn't reek this bad.

When they reached the main apartment door, Charlie did her usual lock-picking trick.

Zan smiled. "You have to teach me how to do that sometime," she said.

"Sure, it's not that hard. What is hard are the newer deadbolts. Or those locks with the PIN codes. Those are hard to crack without a device." She opened the door and they walked in.

The smell was stronger inside. They walked up the stairs to the drug dealers' apartment.

This time, Charlie didn't have to pick the door. It was already ajar. Inside, it was chaos. There were dead bodies all over the place.

"Hey, you took your time," called out Stan.

"What the?" exclaimed Zan, entering the room. She looked down at a body on the ground. "Is that John?" she asked.

He nodded. "Yep, our zombie business got a bit out of hand."

Acting as if nothing was out of the ordinary, Charlie flopped down on the couch. "So, what's up?" she asked. She looked around the room, but it appeared that the six dead zombies on the floor of the apartment were actually dead.

"Well, see here," began Stan. "My partner

and I thought we'd continue Eli's zrug business. But without zombies, we can't make zrug. So, we sourced some out. But things got crazy. One bit John. I couldn't stand it, so I killed the rest of them." He sat down at the other end of the couch. "I guess I'm going to have to get a real job now."

"Wow," said Zan, joining them on the couch. "That's something. Maybe you could join our zombie slayer cause. Usually a civilian can barely tackle one, let alone six."

"Nah," he replied. "I'm done. I'll try and figure out how to make a living and get a job tomorrow."

"OK, so we have a question for you," said Charlie. "Where did you get the zombies from?"

"Oh, that's easy," he said. "I got them from— Hey! Look out behind you!" he yelled.

Charlie quickly turned, wondering what could be behind her, as the couch was close to the wall.

A gunshot rang out. Zan looked horrified. She looked at Stan, who held a smoking gun in his hand. Then she looked at her friend, who had been shot.

She was about to go for Stan when he

dropped the gun. "I was aiming for the zombie. I swear!"

It was true. There was a zombie behind Charlie with its head propped up against the back of the couch. It had a bullet through its skull.

CHAPTER 20

The bullet had sliced through Charlie's left shoulder and gone right through the zombie's eye socket.

Zan floundered around, looking for something to cover the wound.

"Here," yelled Stan, tossing the first-aid kit at her.

Zan quickly tore open the box and applied dressings to both sides. "I think you'll live," she said to Charlie. "It didn't hit a major artery, and the bullet went straight through."

"Still," said Stan, "you'd better seek medical care. There is a hospital right down the street."

"Great," said Charlie. "I'll be fine. Don't worry about me."

"I'll take her," Zan said. "Probably better than calling 911, otherwise, the police will be here and ask questions."

"Hey, that's great. Thank you for thinking of me."

"Well, only because you're going to tell me where to find your zombie supplier."

"Fine," said Stan. He told her the information.

Zan supported Charlie out the door. Stan helped them walk the two blocks to her vehicle. They got her safely inside the car. Stan waved goodbye while Zan drove the car to the hospital.

"Hey," said Zan to the emergency room check-in desk clerk. "I found this girl on the street, shot. She needs help."

An orderly rushed in with a wheelchair.

"Geez," said Charlie. "Talk to you later." But Zan was already gone.

They wheeled her into the ER. She frowned as they cut her favorite top away from her skin. A doctor came and examined her, proclaimed that she would live, but needed stitches. A nurse came by next to clean up the wound. The doctor stitched her up and gave her a shot of antibiotics.

Her body spasmed immediately. "Dammit!" yelled the doctor. "Allergic reaction! Need epi now!"

The nurse handed the syringe to him. He injected it into her arm. Charlie's spasms stopped. She looked up at him, a worried expression plastered on her face.

"We're keeping you here overnight," he said. "Just to make sure you'll be OK."

"Well isn't that just great," Charlie said. She was greatly annoyed that she was missing out on all the fun.

zzz

"1207 West 30th Street," said Zan to herself. "It should be around the hospital. This doesn't make sense. Maybe Stan made a mistake." She sat in Charlie's car, looking at the hospital.

"Oh shit. The source is the hospital! I need my fellow zlayer!" Zan drove the car back to the hospital's parking lot. She rushed to the emergency check-in counter. "Where's Charlie Warner?" she asked the clerk.

"Let's see. Charlie has been admitted. She is in room 3A."

Zan raced around the counter and down

the hallway. "3A. 3A. 3A," she said frantically. She found it and threw open the door.

"Hey, Zan," said Charlie. "How nice of you to come by for a visit," she said sarcastically.

"Hey, sorry for bailing. I wanted to find the zombie suppliers as quickly as possible."

"Any luck?"

"Why yes! Wait, what's happened to you? I thought they'd release you today."

"Nope. It turns out that I'm allergic to the antibiotic. They want to keep an eye on me for today. I'll be out tomorrow morning."

"Whew," said Zan. "That's good news. Now, I have some news too. I've got the address where the zombies are being held and created."

"Oh yeah?" asked Charlie.

"It's right here at the hospital," she explained.

"Are you serious?" said Charlie in amazement.

"Yep. I expect something is going on right under our noses. Literally," she said, peering down at the ground.

"Down in the morgue?" asked Charlie. Zan nodded.

"OK, get down there and see if you can destroy them," said Charlie.

"On it," said Zan, proud of herself for figuring out what was happening.

She raced down the hallway and to the stairs. At the very bottom of the staircase was a large metal door. She tried to turn the knob, but it was locked. She leaned sideways and then kicked her foot out. The knob fell off the door. "Works every time," she said, feeling quite pleased with herself. "Who needs lock picking?"

She opened the door and found another hallway. She walked down it. The morgue had to be here somewhere. It was always in the basement, so it was kept far away from the living.

Finally, in the distance, she saw a huge sign that said MORGUE on it, like it was necessary to advertise what was inside the room.

She peered through the glass windows at the top of the double doors. There was no one inside. She pushed the doors open. It wasn't locked. But then, who would steal bodies? Perhaps criminals who hoped to profit off the dead.

She entered the room. Ahead of her were

three exam tables and about thirty refrigerator doors. She started on her right. Might as well get this done. The first few yielded no bodies. The next three did. She couldn't be certain about their stage of decomposition. She decided to play it safe and rammed her dagger through their eye sockets and into their skulls. Even if someone tried to reanimate them, they would not succeed. She pushed the gurneys back in and closed the doors. The next set of doors revealed nothing. She looked back at the main doors. She should have time to examine all of them.

This was the only solution she could thing of. That and possibly wait until the guilty party entered the room. On the other hand, she guessed that many people probably had access to the morgue. Perhaps the best thing she could do was to destroy the corpses, and then try and find out how they were being reanimated.

zzz

Back in her room, Charlie started feeling

strange. She felt a bit lightheaded and brain dead.

"How are we doing today?" asked the same doctor who had given her the dose of antibiotics earlier.

"A bit weird, dizzy."

"Oh, that's normal after an allergic reaction. Get some rest, and you'll feel much better tomorrow." He left the room. There was something creepy about that doctor, but she couldn't put her finger on it.

She wondered if meal service started soon. She could eat a nice raw steak at the moment.

zzz

Zan had finally gone through and destroyed all the corpses' brains. There. No one would be using any of these bodies to create zombies and make zrugs.

She heard a noise in the distance. "Where to hide, where to hide?" she muttered to herself.

The door opened. "I could have sworn I heard noise in here," said one orderly to another.

"All looks fine," said the other guy.

"This room creeps me out. I swear Dr. Fisher is up to no good sometimes," said the first guy.

"You mean, he might be making drugs on the side or something?" He had a good laugh.

"Yeah, you never know."

"Well, what I don't like is that all these people are getting allergic reactions to an antibiotic, and then dying. Doesn't make sense."

"That is unusual. Let's keep an eye on it. We might have to report it."

The two orderlies left the room. Zan could hear their footsteps heading down the hallway.

"Shit! Antibiotics!" she yelled. She pushed against the fridge door and it opened. Good thing it opened on both sides, otherwise, she'd be permanently cooled. She jumped out, and then closed the door. She padded over to the main doors and looked out. No one was around.

She threw open the doors and raced down the hallway. She ran up the stairs and back to room 3A. She flung open the door to Charlie's room, but she wasn't there. Surprised, she found a nurse tearing the sheets off the bed.

"Where is Charlie Warner?" asked Zan, panicking.

"Oh, dear. I'm sorry," said the nurse. "She didn't make it. The orderlies took her away on the gurney."

Zan raced down the hallway. They would be heading for the elevator. She watched as the indicator slowly changed to B. She found the stairwell at that end of the hospital and raced down to the basement. They had to be taking her to the morgue.

Ahead she saw a man, who appeared to be a doctor, wheeling the gurney to the morgue.

She raced up to him. "Excuse me, she's not dead," said Zan.

The doctor looked up and stopped moving. "Of course not," said the doctor. "There's a reason why I need her alive." He went back to pushing on the gurney. He pushed it straight through the swinging doors of the morgue. Zan followed them in.

Inside, the doctor pulled out a gun.

"So, it's you who's been making zombies!' said Zan, realizing that he was likely the source of all the zombie issues for the past few months.

The doctor had a smug expression on his face. "Oh yes," he said. "I started out helping Eli to make the zrug from zombie brains. Might as well make some profits on the side, right? Then I decided to infect the Portland High School students. I worked with Steve, John, and Stan, though that last guy is weak. I set up the zombie wedding at the mansion. I convinced John to sell zombies to the fashion show. I tried to infect the students at the dance, but that drug I sold those kids was ineffective and did nothing. I've been experimenting for a long time now."

Zan looked at him and the gun in his hand.

"I've finally perfected the zrug. I'm going to make millions of dollars. And, I can quickly and easily infect as many people as I need." He raised his gun and aimed.

The shot rang out.

Zan dropped to the ground. She'd learned to dodge more than a few bullets in her time.

The doctor aimed the gun again. But this time, no shots rang out. She took this opportunity and leapt out at him. She raised her dagger in her hand and plunged it into his eye socket. As she did so, she saw a contact lenses slip out of his other eye. Beneath, his eye glowed green.

Zan ran to Charlie and removed the titanium dagger from inside her hospital gown. She ran back, plunged it into Dr. Fisher's other eye socket, and recited the spell, "Reliqua autem impius!" That stopped the glow. The zleader dropped to the ground.

Zan ran over to Charlie and slapped her cheeks. Her eyes opened.

"Hey, you OK?" she asked.

"Yep," said Charlie. "That was one hell of a dream."

Zan quickly dragged his corpse into one of the fridge slots before cleaning up. She then wheeled Charlie back to the main floor of the hospital.

"Such incompetence," she said to the nursing station. "She is alive." The nurses rushed to the gurney, wheeling Charlie back to her room.

A new doctor showed up, one that could be trusted.

"I'm so sorry, Miss Warner. That doctor

has had some complaints on his record. We have been destroying any and all antibiotics that he's been administering to patients. I'll be sure to report him to the authorities."

The doctor gave Charlie a clean bill of health, but said she'd still have to stay overnight.

Zan decided to stay and make sure that no further incidents happened. She called Stewart, Owen, and Gran to let them know what was going on.

"That's crazy," said Charlie, when Zan told her about the doctor. "I've been a zlayer for almost two years and I have never ever seen zombie plagues occur at such a rapid pace."

"I know," said Zan. "Turns out that something was up after all. Imagine, making real zombies."

They had a good chuckle over that.

EPILOGUE

Charlie relaxed in her hospital bed. They'd given her just enough painkillers to dampen the pain in her shoulder, but not enough to make her brain too foggy.

She heard footsteps outside the hospital room. She closed her eyes.

"Shhh," someone said. "She's still out. We should let her rest and come back tomorrow." The footsteps left.

Relieved, she opened her eyes. She'd see everyone tomorrow. She was so glad that her friends had survived. This time she hadn't lost anyone.

Then there were more footsteps to her room, probably the nurse to check on her.

"Hey, time to get up. They're discharging you today," said Stewart.

She opened her eyes. "Fine," she said.

"You feeling all right?"

She nodded. "Where's Gran?"

"She's at home preparing your room," he explained. "I promised her I'd bring you back home."

She sat up in bed, feeling a bit woozy.

"Take it easy," he said.

"So, is everything back to normal now?" she asked. "I can really retire?"

"Yes, you can really retire from zombie slaying. How ironic that Doctor Fisher laid a false trail of zleaders for us to find. I should have known something was up every time they'd spring up somewhere else."

He tucked her jacket around her since there was no way she'd be able to put her left arm into the jacket's sleeve. Then he helped her into the wheelchair that the nurse rolled in. He pushed her out of her room to the front desk, where she signed out.

Feeling strong enough, Charlie was able to stand up and they walked down the long corridor to the parking lot. The hospital was quiet at this time of day. They quickly found his car and he drove her home.

She breathed a sigh of relief.

"Now, I know you've retired from zombie slaying, and it'll take some time for the bullet wound to heal up, but hear what I have to say."

"What is it?" she asked him.

"Well, word has it that zombies are loose in Seattle."

"What?" she said. "Wait, someone went to Seattle recently. Who was it?" She pondered the thought.

"Yep. Apparently, that's where the next outbreak is," said Stewart.

"Wait a minute. I think it was the owner of The Bean Trip."

"You mean that coffee shop that burned down on Main Street?"

She nodded. "Yes, before Steve died he told me that the owner had fled to Seattle. He was tired of his life of crime."

"Oh," he said. "So, this means one of two things. One, he was bitten before he fled. Or two, he took some of the zrug with him that Doctor Fisher had made."

"Wait, can he use the zrug to make more zombies?"

"I'm not certain. I'm a mentor and biology teacher, not a scientist. But with some of the things that have happened in the last few years, I wouldn't be surprised."

"Great. So we'll have to figure it out," she said.

"Yep. Wait a minute, are you coming to Seattle with me?" he asked.

She sat back in the seat. "I'm not saying anything. First, I want my stupid shoulder to heal up." Then her eyes opened wide. "When we were holding Tonia in Zan's backyard, she said that Owen was immune to zombie bites."

Stewart and Charlie looked at each other. Perhaps they would be better prepared for the next zombie outbreak. Maybe retirement could wait.

***

She thought she left it all behind. But morbid hellspawn aren't content to chill in the parking lot after school.

Start reading Second Strain to find out what happens to Charlie and her zombie-slaying friends next! **Grab it at BooksByGayle.com**

***

Hungry for more? Claim your zombie short story collection when you sign-up for Gayle's newsletter at **GayleKatz.com/3zombies**

A NOTE FROM GAYLE

Thanks for reading my book! Life as a zombie slayer is a complicated one. So is being a writer, editor, proofreader and coordinating the cover design, book formatting, promotions, and everything else that goes into bringing a book to market as a one-person publishing company. The fact that you took the time to read my book out of all the ones out there makes me smile. Yep, I'm beaming!

With all that said, I write because of our collective hunger for intense zombie adventures that reach out and grab us!

If you enjoyed the story, please take a few minutes to write a review. Your review helps other readers to find a book they'll love! If you leave a review, I would love to read it! Email me a copy of the review or a link to it at **gayle@gaylekatz.com**

Hop onto your computer, tablet, or phone and type in BooksByGayle.com, find *Charlie*, and click the "Write A Customer Review" button.

And you can stay up-to-date on upcoming releases and sales by joining my newsletter at **GayleKatz.com/3zombies**

ABOUT GAYLE KATZ

Gayle is a fan of zombies, sci-fi fantasy, and psychological horror—though not necessarily in that order.

She writes the kinds of books she wants to read but often can't find. Hoping to scare you, make you swoon, and root for her characters, her love of kick-butt heroines and sassy snark shines through in her work.

Born and raised outside of Philadelphia, Pennsylvania, Gayle discovered her passion for zombies when her husband introduced her to video games in 2009. Gayle writes about the undead because they scare the bejesus out of her and she likes it!

MORE STORIES FOR YOU
TO DISCOVER

ZOMBIE SLAYER: a young adult dystopian horror - A fast-paced, horror suspense series packed with zombie hordes, sassy slayers, and a touch of the supernatural

JANE ZOMBIE CHRONICLES: a post-apocalyptic horror - A first-hand account: desperate to overcome my insecurities and fit in, I fight for my life and the lives of my fellow survivors in a zombie apocalypse threatening to annihilate all of humanity.

TEARS OF VENUS: an end-of-the-world, sci-fi adventure trilogy - The government is hiding a secret. Charlotte knows the answers are a world away. When disaster strikes, will she get off the ground or pay with her life?

THE SILENT CELLS: a psychological horror - Resources are running low. People are desperate. Crime is on the rise. But Dolores is innocent.

Visit BooksByGayle.com to read more stories by Gayle!

CONTINUE THE ADVENTURE!

Here's your special SNEAK PEEK from the second book in the Zombie Slayer series, *Second Strain*.

She sat up straight when she heard a sound coming from behind her car. She tossed her garbage back into the paper bag and tossed it on the floor of the car. She carefully patted her back jeans pocket, the one that had been altered to safely fit her dagger so she didn't stab her butt.

Whatever it was moving around behind her car made rattling sounds. She slowly opened the passenger side door and got out.

A dark figure loomed in front of her. His hands reached for her neck, while his jaws chomped up and down. As he got closer, he slowly dragged one foot after the other. She just stood there watching him, with a bored expression on her face.

The creature came closer. His eyes glowed green. He stuck out his tongue, and then bit it off. The tip fell into his hands. He placed the tongue back in his mouth and swallowed.

"Really?" she asked. "How will you moan?"

The zombie was now right beside her. She pulled out her dagger and quickly plunged it into his eye socket. The body dropped quickly to the ground. She quickly sheathed her dagger.

Then her skin twitched. She abruptly looked around in all directions and used her key to open the hatchback of her classic car. She quickly grabbed onto the male body and pulled him into the back.

"Oof," she said. "Must do more weightlifting. There."

The body was in the back of her car. She slammed the door shut. Just as she was glancing at the ground for blood to clean up, something struck her head. Her body slammed against her car, and then she slipped to the ground. She tried to fight and maintain her consciousness, but someone or something picked her up and carried her into the back seat of a car.

Will Charlie survive, or are her zombie-slaying days numbered?

Visit BooksByGayle.com to check out Second Strain, the next book in the Zombie Slayer series.